FOX TALES

PART 1 ANCESTRAL QUEST

by

P. D. Shaun

DORRANCE
PUBLISHING CO
EST. 1920
PITTSBURGH, PENNSYLVANIA 15238

Dorrance Publishing Co
585 Alpha Drive
Pittsburgh, PA 15238
Visit our website at *www.dorrancebookstore.com*

ISBN: 978-1-6442-6442-3
eISBN: 978-1-6442-6099-9

Fox Tales

Part 1 Ancestral Quest

by

P. D. Shaun

As I lay there on the ground looking up at the blue lit sky. I could not help myself but to think that I have been to this place before, but something was different about this place. The blue that lite the sky was the only light around. There was no sun or moon to be found. The wind blew, and I could hear the trees' branches rattling and leaves shaking, but I could not sense any forms of life. I could not smell any magic in the air. Smelling magic has been an art the Foxfang have known since the beginning of time. Not all tribe members are born with it, and some sense the smell of magic more than others.

I picked myself off the ground and looked behind me to see a village of tree dwellings remarkably similar to my tribe, if not the same. As I walked past the trees, I noticed the placing of the dwellings were the same as my village, but there was no one around. No young cubs running around. No men training in the fields. No women tending to crops. The whole village, not a soul.

I headed towards where my tree would be in my village. As I approached its massive trunk with a spiral set of stairs that wrapped around it, and up to the top is where my hut would be. I began to count the steps as I walked up; because I built these steps and my hut myself, I have walked up and down them since I was young. I ran my hand up, digging my nails into the bark. I always would do this if I were in a hurry. As I got closer to the top, I started to think to myself, *Have I died and met the Maker? Or even somewhere in Obrix's Realm … …?*

I reached the top; there was exactly 107 steps, the same as on my dwelling. Before I entered the hut, I shouted out: "Hello! Where is everyone?"

No reply came from inside the hut.

I pushed open the door and walked in. Looking around, and the only thing I could see was blue flames in the fireplace in the corner of the room and two walls full of ancient tomes and maps. This was my hut, but none of my fittings were to be found. The flames were blue, but I could not sense any magic.

How was that possible? My sense of magic smelling could pick up a wind spell being casted the next village over, but to not smell blue flames in front of my very eyes led me to believe something I had no control over was going on. Could I be dead? Or had someone drained me of my powers?

I walked over to the bookshelf to where my favorite book would be. I picked up *The Ancient Art of Blade Handling*, but when I opened it, the pages were empty. I grabbed the book next to it, and again the pages were bare.

I grabbed another, and another, and they were all the same. Books with titles but not a word on any page. I walked over to the fireplace and examined the flames. I looked at them for a moment and noticed that they were not giving off any heat. How could this be?

Thuum!

I heard a noise in the distance and felt the ground shake.

Thuum!

The noise was getting closer and louder. I ran out the hut and jumped on top to see what was coming my way.

Thud!

The trees were crashing and hit the ground. From the top of the hut, I could only see the shine of its armor. The blue light in the sky blinded me as it reflected off its armor. The shiny creature started to run faster towards me. I braced myself for combat, not knowing if it was friend or foe. It came out of the tree line, and I could finally see what it was rumbling the earth beneath me. It was an enormous suit of silver armor, it wielded a giant two-handed sword that looked like not even 10 men could carry it. The boots were long as river boats. It stood almost as tall as all the surrounding trees. The engraving design on the armor was nothing like I had seen before. It had to have been royal or high-ranking general armor. As I made contact with its eyes, there were no eyes. Just very dim blue flames; the same as the ones in the fireplace.

We both stood still, then held its sword in one hand and pointed it at me.

"You the one they call Zek of the Foxfang?" It spoke in a deep voice that echoed inside the hollow suite of armor. How it knew this information about me, I did not know.

"I am Zek! Who might you be stranger?" I replied with balled fist and blood boiling.

"I am the one they call Roztig King of the Silver Giants."

I could not believe I was staring in the face of a legendary warrior that was only mentioned in folk tales and bedtime stories for young ones. I did not believe these stories to be true until now.

Silver Giants were the armor of once living men, whose souls have moved on to the afterlife, but their spirit to fight kept the armor alive. Some taller than others. The more a dying man wanted to fight, the taller it would be. That made them grow to such towering heights that most would not even attempt to cross paths with them nor blades, and here I found myself standing face-to-face with King Roztin. His armor was magnificent; it looked as if it was forged by the Maker himself.

"What is it that you want?" I demanded an answer from the towering giant.

"It is quite simple. I am here for your head."

A smile found its way to my face. What are the chances I could have angered the King of the Silver Giants? My smile angered Roztig, and he growled and gripped his sword tighter.

Preparing myself for combat, I took to the Foxfang fighting stance. My fox claws came out, sharp as daggers. The hair on the back of my neck stood up like needles. I let out the Howl for War.

Foxfang were mostly half half-fox and half half-human creatures. Some had more fox than human than others. Me personally, there was more fox to me than human. My ears, nose, feet, hands, and tail were all fox. The only thing human about me was the skin on my chest, my arms, legs and the hair on my head. Which I wore in locks. I grew up with a cub who was all human, and the only thing that was fox about him was his feet. We stood up and walked on two feet, but a few of us walked around on all fours. We were often confused with werewolves, but we are not filthy beasts nor damn savages like them.

I let Roztig make the first move. He charged me and swung his sword swiftly at the tree I was standing on. I jumped back before he could hit me. His mighty swing split a tree in half and brought it crashing to the ground. Landing my two feet on the ground, I went for him. Running as fast I could, I lunged at him and started to claw where his heart would be if he had one. I barely grazed his armor, it was as if you tried to dig your nails into a stone. Kicking him in his chest moved him back very little but sent me flying in the other direction. Coming at me for a second swing, this time he swung sideways as if he were going to take off my head. Jumping before he could reach me, I landed on the end of his blade, and bracing myself for another attack, I jumped off his swords backwards and cast my *fox fire*. This angered Roztig greatly.

A burst of magical flames that was shaped like the head of a fox. Aimed for his helm. My *fox fire* landed, but the flames did not stay lit for long. When the flames cleared, he let out a mighty roar, and the blue flames in his helm grew larger as he stood there. Larger and larger, until they shot out at me. Trapped by flames on both sides, I rolled out of his eyesight and darted into the forest as fast as I could to find a large tree to hide behind to think of my next move. As I stood there panting trying to catch a breather, I could hear him smashing trees and calling out to me.

"Have you had enough yet, Foxfang? We've just started, and I have not yet to begun having fun with you."

While trying to catch my breath, I tried to remember my teachings about these legendary creatures, but the only thing that came to mind is how I thought they were not real, and I never paid attention to my grandpa and how to kill them. Hearing the footsteps getting closer, I climbed up the tree I was hiding behind and jumped into the air to hit him with more *fox fire*. This time putting more focus into each blast so that I could actually slow him down and do some damage. I landed on the ground and heard him shout: "Is that all you got, Foxfang?"

As the flames moved away from his body, I could see that his armor was not as shiny anymore. Was I doing harm to him, or was I just throwing more oil on the fire? I pulled out my sword Judgment. This sword was given to me by my father. He gave it that name because of the way he lived his life. Treat every person with respect. Their actions will judge them you do not need. Never use Judgment on anyone.

He laughed as I pulled out my sword. Maybe he was expecting me to run, but I did not. Standing my ground, he swung, but I blocked his blow. He hit me with so much force that my feet dug into the ground. He came in for another blow. I parried his attack and placed myself behind him. Jumping up, I began to slash his back. I was greeted by a blind elbow Roztig threw behind his back. When it landed, it sent me sailing through the trees. Before I could pick myself up off the ground, I saw him dropping his big boot towards my face. Blocking it as best I could, this massive step dug me deeper into the ground. As he lifted his foot up, I hit him with another blast of *fox fire* under his foot. This sent him flying, and he landed on his back. Taking full advantage of this opportunity, leaping up and thrusting my sword into his heart. My blade went in point deep; not deep enough to do any damage. He punched my mid-section, but the top of his fist hit the tip of my chin. It was like trying to catch a boulder coming down a mountain.

Roztig pulled my sword out of his chest and threw it into a tree. He threw it, with so much force, it made a hole in the tree and then stuck into a stone. He saw my eyes look towards my sword as I made a dash to try to get it. He swung his sword faster than I could grab mine. If he would have landed that one I probably would have been missing a hand. I hit him with more *fox fire* in his face so that I could try to pull out my sword, but it was in there very snug. As the flames cleared his helm, it lost some more shine; it seemed as if I was doing more and more damage to him. I could not tell because he was still hitting me with what had seemed like everything he had. We stood there looking at each other in the face both breathing heavy.

"Yes. You are the one," he whispered. What he meant by this; I did not know.

He threw his sword into the ground, and it shook the earth beneath me. He put his large, clenched hands up as if he wanted to settle this like men. He swung at me; I dodged and landed two punches. He swung again and landed this time. He swung again, this time faster, and the one that followed that one was even faster. Until it came to the point where I was dodging a few of his hits and taking a blow to the face or to the side. How could a creature so big have fists that moved so swiftly? Once again, we stood looking at each other out

of breath, still wanting to fight, still wanting to put an end to one another. By looking at him, it seemed he could barely lift his fist for another attack. Was this the reason why he dropped his sword? Was I giving him a run for his coin? Or was he a crazed madman who wanted to take my life with his bare hands?

Readying myself for another attack, I puffed up my chest and let out an ear pounding howl. My fists were balled so tight, my nails pierced my skin. The ground beneath me cracked; the air was no longer still, and the wind blew under me picking me up in the air.

Roztig seemed shocked to see me in the air and to see so much power come from me, but while this was happening, he had a smile on his face the whole time. Maybe he knew his end was coming, or maybe he was looking for this fight the whole time. I'd never seen this much power come from me; it was like I found some new energy from within. We charged each other again. This time, we had matching fists of swiftness. Hitting one another so hard that it just made us hit each other harder. I managed to stop his punches by digging my nails and grabbing both of his boulder-like fists. As he tried to get his hands free, I laughed, "Is that all you got?"

I was in control of his hands. I slowly overpowered him and turned his writs. Sending his hands to the ground violently brought his head closer to mine. Then delivering him a head-butt that sent him off into the trees I stood still. I think I may have dented his helm, but I do believe that hurt me more than it hurt him. Picking himself out of the trees, I could hear him shout.

"Yes, Foxfang, this is what I've been waiting for. Now your head is mine!"

At that moment, Roztig began to glow, a brighter silver than he already was. The flames in his eyes grew bigger and bigger; he was getting ready for his last showing of will. He came charging at me with both hands grasped together. With both hands together, he jumped in the air and came down with his hammer fist. I was able to dodge this attack, but the hole he left in the ground looked like three hill giants fell from the sky. This landed me right next to my sword, but as I tried to grab for it again, he came down with another hammer fist. So, I darted towards his sword to see if I could pull it out of the ground. To my surprise, I pulled it out with ease. How was this possible? Was it from the burst of energy I got, or was this sword just all about looks: big and intimidating, but with no real power to it?

Without thinking another thought, I swung the sword wildly and sliced off his right arm. This did not stop him from coming at me; he still punched me with his left so hard, there was no more breath in me. As I laid there on the ground, the next thing I saw was the arm I just cut off come for me. The hand opened up and wrapped itself around me; my arms were unable to move, and I could feel its grip getting tighter. Roztig stuck his still-connected hand out, and his sword came to it. The cut off arm had me in the air and pressed to a tree. Roztig was walking towards me. As he was walking towards me, he began to speak to me with a sense of joy in voice.

"You see here, Foxfang, I told you I would have your head." He began to laugh as he continued to approach me. "Your all was just not enough, Foxfang."

After those words were spoken, the last I saw was Roztig charge at me with his blade in hand, aiming to take my head off as he spoke of this whole time...

My world went black.

I woke up breathing heavy sweating and screaming. I was just having a dream of fighting the King of the Silver Giants and him cutting my head off. It had all seemed so real to me, and I could not help but to think that dream meant something. Was that a dream of what was to happen, or was that a dream that had a hidden meaning? This bothered me because usually when I have dreams like that, something bad happens. Once I had dreamed I was turned into a werewolf by a witch who knew I was Foxfang and knew how much we hated the honorless beast. In the dream, I was hated by my own people because I was a wolf, and I was hated by the werewolf because I smelled like a fox. Hated by everyone, that is what she wanted, and that's what happened in the dream. Then sometime later, I was attacked by a werewolf and bitten, but I did not turn into one. It left me sick for almost two seasons, but my grandfather watched over me and used all his skills as a wizard to help me not turn. So, how long would it be before I came face-to-face with a Silver Giant?

My grandfather walked in with a look of concern.

He asked, "What seems to be the matter?"

"I had a dream that I fought Roztig, King of the Silver Giants, and he cut my head off. But before he bested me, I gained strength like I had never felt before. What could that have meant?" I replied.

My grandfather, Shadow, was not blood to me at all, but he did raise me and show me the basics of casting spells. He was also accepted by my people; they had trusted him for many generations of Foxfang. It was a little strange that the Foxfangs befriending a wizard turned out to be a wonderful friendship. Shadow was not like other wizards in many ways. Most people think of wizards as tall, wrinkle-faced old men with pointy hats, gray hair, and long beards. Shadow did have hair on his head, but it is not long. It is white and barely poked out of his hat. He did have a long beard, but it was white, not gray. Shadow's skin is very dark. When the sun graced him, he would often shine. He has amazing skin no wrinkles. Shadow's face looked as if he had been in manhood for quite some time now, but he was well over 100 years old. Some thought he drank from the Fountain of Youth; others thought he was under someone's spell or cursed. He was a shadow wizard dressed in a white pointed hat with white robes. Many people who did not know of him thought he was of the clergy because he dressed himself in all white. Shadow wizards could take the form of anything that casted a shadow, and they could also control the shadows. Shadow element spell casters were very rarely seen because they would either take the form of some other shadow or just stay away from others. You would think them to live in the dark, but a shadow cannot live in complete darkness.

"That sounds like quite the dream, my son. It's interesting to hear you dreamed of someone who you have never met. I am also interested in what would possess the king himself of legendary creatures to come find you."

Shadow was a very wise man; any information he would receive, he would sunder upon it until he could wrap his mind around it. When he was not around people, he was either reading a book or writing one.

"But what I am most of all curious about, my son," he continued, "is the energy that you speak of. Can you explain it to me more"?

"Where do I start? My muscles tightened up like I never felt before. My speed was lighting fast, swift, and close to unnoticeable. I went into like a transformation where all I wanted to do was fight. The more I fought, the more I swung, the more my fist pounded and dented his armor, the happier I was."

That was the best way I could explain what had happened to me in my dream. Shadow walked over to the window and folded his arms behind his back. As he looked out the window, he let out a sigh and said, "Zek, trance is the right word for that. I haven't heard of a Foxfang going into a trance since the time of your father's father Zelk and his four sons were able to slip in and out of a trance when they wanted to. Somehow, they could control that amount of power. Others before them when Foxfang would go into a trance as you described, they wanted to fight more and more. Their fists breaking bones and claws clawing flesh made them happy. Cutting their heads off was the only way to stop them."

As I listened to his words, I realized that Roztig cut my head off in the dream because I was in a trance, and he knew that I had bested him. If I could have controlled myself while in the trance, maybe I would have killed him before he could even draw his sword, but it was only a dream. I told myself that over and over, but somehow I had the feeling that that dream was a nightmare, or soon to be reality.

"Father, do you know of any way to control your powers while in a trance?"

"I have not dealt with the art of going into a trance. Going into a trance is something only Foxfang can do. We should go talk to Zemu. Maybe he could tell you more about the matter than I can."

Elder Zemu was not the strongest of the Foxfang, but he was the wisest. We did not believe in alpha males or pack leaders, hand to hand combat or killing to become the leader like the werewolves of the world. We believed that our leader should be wise and strong in the mind. Anyone could bulk up and gain muscles, but only a few would ever bulk up in the mind. We were extraordinarily strong and gifted warriors, but our minds were our most powerful weapons. Elder Zemu was the only one in the tribe that did not stay at the top of a tree hut. The elders' huts were on the ground in the middle of the village surrounded by all their kinsmen of the tribe.

As we left my hut to head to Elder Zemu, I asked Shadow, "Do you think Elder Zemu will have the answers we seek?"

"He will be able to answer your questions better than I. I'm sure he was around at the time the last group of Foxfangs went into a trance."

As we continued walking, I wondered if Elder Zemu was around at that time. He would only have been a tod. How would he have known anything about a trance? I kept my questions to myself as we walked to Elder Zemu's hut.

As we approached the hut, Elder Zemu was sitting outside reading a book. I could only make out one word: Fury.

"Ahh, Master Shadow, Zek! What brings you to see my sad sack of bones?"

"Zek here has had a very vivid dream about going into a trance," said Shadow.

"How interesting, I have heard whispers here and there. I was sensing a trance, but definitely not from you," he said as he waved the book in my face. "So, the son of the outcast, D'zjoe, is the one I've been sensing."

My father was an outcast; most everyone in the tribe did not take me seriously. He went mad before he was cast out from the village. He spoke of being the legendary Night Fox. Although he never showed proof of it, some believed him, and others thought him as a babbling fool.

"If this is to be true, young Zek, there is only one way to find out if you possess the ability," Elder Zemu said. "Drink the blood of the Night Fox and enter." As he spoke those words, he lifted a large rock inside his hut and pointed into a dark hole. The hole was not very deep; it looked as if it could only fit a curled-up body, and it would squish a body if the rock was set down.

"Elder Zmu, are you sure he is ready for such a thing?" Shadow asked the question and had a look on his face as if he saw a ghost. "If he is not the one there is a chance he may die down there."

My face, too, began to look as if I saw the same ghost when I heard the possibility of me dying.

Elder Zemu replied, "Be that as it may, other Foxfangs have tried this ritual many times. Many of Foxfangs have died, and many have emerged without the ability to go in to a trance but have lived to tell what they have saw from drinking the blood of the Night Fox."

It was only a dream, I thought to myself. I had no idea that me having such a vivid dream could lead to me dying this early in the morning.

"Shall we enter?" Shadow asked.

"No, Master Shadow, you may not. The Foxfang ritual, only the Foxfang shall enter."

"I can do this, Father," I said to Shadow. I looked at Elder Zemu. He nodded and handed me a cup that had a thick, dark red liquid in it, almost black. I had never tasted blood before; holding this cup made me think of all the times we youngsters thought that the blood of the Night Fox was the name of a potion the elders made up. But here in front of me now, I knew it was truly blood.

"I always thought this ritual to be myth, but here before my very eyes, I witness these events," Shadow said to the elder.

"Master Shadow, the ritual of the Night Fox has been around for many generations. One of three things happen when you drink from this cup. You will find the energy that you seek inside you to see, if your body possesses the power to go into a trance. You will see the Night Fox…" Elder Zemu paused. "Or you will hallucinate and die. Are you sure you want to do this Zek?"

"Elder Zemu, the dream I had about the trance seemed so real, my body has to be able to go into a trance. How could I have a vivid dream about something I have no knowledge about? That's got to mean something."

I began to drink from the cup. The liquid was thick and bitter. I made my way over to the large rock. Then while laying down in the hole, I heard Elder Zemu chant something in ancient Foxfang tongue. He then began to lower the rock on top of me while still chanting. Moments later, everything was dark, and I could no longer hear the chanting. Complete darkness and silence were the only things surrounding me.

As time went by, I thought maybe I was misled into drinking a foul tasting liquid, and I was made a fool of to sit in a hole with a large rock on top of me. I waited a while longer, then I began to get angry. That old bastard hoaxed me. I pushed on the rock, and to my surprise, it moved. I gave it my all, and the rock was no longer on top of me, but when I poked my head out, I was no longer in Elder Zemu's hut. I arose in a place that was full of Foxfang bones and fog. This must have been

the bones of the other Foxfang who did not make it. There was a long trail of steps that led to a temple in the middle of the mountain. The sun was very bright, but the air was cold, as if it was morning time in the spring. There was a lot of death surrounding this place, but everything seemed very calm. It was not gloomy or depressing. I felt at peace and at home in this place.

I started walking my way towards the temple to see what lay in store for me there. As I made my way there, I noticed more and more bones. Bones as far as the eye could see, mountains of bones. Many of my Foxfang brethren must of drank from the cup, but it also looked like many did not make it. This ritual must have been going on for a very long time, I could not imagine a person willing to give their life for power or a chance to see the Night Fox. Yet I found myself here not knowing what would come of it. Arriving at the temple doors, I noticed the doors were made of extraordinary large fox teeth. The fox that these came from must have been a towering giant. I took a deep breath and pushed the doors open.

Opening the door, I realized that this temple was spectacular. The inside looked more like a castle than a temple. There were pillars of ivory that went to the ceiling, they had old Foxfang tongue carved into them. The side walls were covered in many years of Foxfang weapons and armor, some so ancient I had never laid eyes on many of them. There was a painting of a large black fox with white eyes. The back wall of the temple had the furs of white foxes, and in front of the wall sat a large, stone throne. Beside the throne sat two, large ivory statues of foxes sitting on their tails. I had never seen such craftsmanship from Foxfang. I walked into the middle of the room and found myself staring at the vast walls. Suddenly, the painting of the fox above me turned into a black cloud of smoke. The cloud of smoke whipped around the room. It spiraled around my arms and legs and then made its way to the throne. The work of art that was above my head moments ago was a real-life creature curled up, sitting in front of me. I noticed that this fox had three tails; the tails were covering its body, so that all that was shown was a set of white eyes.

In a deep voice, the fox said to me, "Another one of my children coming to me seeking answers?"

At that moment, I realized I was talking to the Night Fox himself.

I stood in silence. I was amazed to be face-to-face with a legendary warrior. All the stories that I heard as a child about what he looked like were untrue.

"Speak up, boy! I haven't all day," he roared at me, but his body didn't budge.

"I am Zek, son of..."

Before I could finish, the Night Fox interrupted.

"You are High Born son of D'jzoe?"

"Yes, I am son of D'jzoe. No, I'm not High Born. He was an outcast from the village where I am from."

The Night Fox laughed; I did not find anything to be funny.

"He was said to be mad and was calling himself the Night Fox, so they casted him out?" I explained.

The Night Fox caught his breath. "The Night Fox he is. Mad he is not. I myself came to him and told him he was my great-great-great grandchild, and I needed him to journey to my tomb. It seems that some grave robbing bandits have been going there for quite some time now and taking my bones and making weapons out of them. This I asked of him quite some time ago, and it seems he has not been able to complete the task. So, the burden falls on to you. I would do it myself, but I haven't heard of a sorcerer who wielded enough power to bring me back from the grave."

My first thought was, *Shadow could do this*. Then I thought, *Quite the day I'm having*.

I had no idea I was High Born; everyone made me out to be the son of the outcast and never took me serious in any way. I was drinking strange liquids and being set off on journeys before I even had breakfast.

"But my son, you have traveled the Spine of the Night Fox and into the Temple of the Night Fox. You must of came here for something. Speak your mind freely."

"I have come to you to see if my body possesses the power to go into a trance."

Once again, laughter was his response, and once again, I found nothing funny.

"You would be the first son of mine who could not go into a trance."

Hearing those words put a smile on my face. I too began to laugh. I am High Born; it would be me making a joke out of myself if I could not go into a trance.

"Now, my son, let us see what you got my pup. Move me from this seat."

I began to summon a *fox fire* spell. Focusing myself, I gave it everything I had and sent it his way. The Night Fox did not move a hair.

"Again!" he shouted. This time, I powered up and sent two blasts. Still, he did not move. I gave it everything my body had to give. "AGAIN!" he shouted.

Running towards him as fast as I could, I combined my *fox fire* with a punch. The punch landed on his face, and the flames nearly melted the stone throne. Once again, he did not budge. I stood there looking at him, out of breath and panting. He uncurled himself from his position and stood on all fours. I was standing face-to-face with the Night Fox. One of his eyes was as big as my head. All I could see was my reflection in his white eyes.

Growling, he said to me, "My son, you have great potential!" He took the form of a cloud of smoke and entered my nose. "Let me show you how to use your powers!"

At that moment, my eyes lit up, I felt his heartbeat pulse through every corner of my body. My muscles tightened up as if they were about to rip through my skin. I was in a trance. The earth began to shake beneath my feet. I no longer was in control of my body. The Night Fox was in control and was getting my body ready to cast *fox fire*.

He placed my feet on the ground firmly, lifted my right arm, and let out a mighty blast. The head of the fox from my fox fire ripped the top of the throne off and sent it through the temple wall. The ground around me was melted away. The ground beneath the blast looked as if someone had dug up the earth. When the smoke cleared, I noticed that he took a chunk out of a mountain in the distance. I had no idea my body had this much power trapped inside. The smoke left my body and took the form of the Night Fox again.

"Ahh, it always feels good to stretch these old bones!" He had a smile on his face and a glow like a playful tod who had just got a treat.

My mind must have been playing tricks on me. Never had I seen someone use that much power. If he would have been sitting on the throne when I shot that one, he would be nothing but a pile of dust.

"The power is in you. It is up to you to find it."

The Night Fox took in a deep breath and blew into my face.

I woke from the hallucination. Shadow and Zemu were looking into my face with eyes as wide as an Opal Owl. Words could not express the looks on the faces they were giving me. The boulder that covered the hole was in pieces around me.

"Did you meet the Night Fox? What did he say? What did you see?" Shadow continued to ask me questions.

I was surprised. I saw all these things but could not believe them. I was sleeping and crumbled a large rock that was on top of me. I was shown power hidden inside of me. I was told I was High Born and shared the same blood as the Night Fox himself. This was much too much for me to take in.

"I did meet the Night Fox. He was nothing like the stories you told when I was younger. He told me bandits are entering his tomb and that I should stop them from making weapons of his bones."

"What about your trance?" the elder asked.

"The Night Fox entered my body and showed me my full potential of *fox fire*."

Elder Zemu had a look on his face like he did not want to hear a word I was saying. I answered all their questions, but I did not tell them I was High Born. I wanted them to know that I could return the bones of our ancient elder before I gave that information.

The tomb of the Night Fox is located in the Grey Mountains. I had never been there, only read about it in books. The Grey Mountains is a place that was home to giants, trolls, thieving and rivaling goblin clans, and all sorts of hermits who wanted to get away from noisy, big market cities and castle life. Dragons patrolled the peaks or guarded their caves full of treasure. Mad Wizards were free to practice spells and experimental potions without burning down half of villages. The Grey Mountains are full of things that could kill you. Somewhere in all that madness was the resting place of the Night Fox.

I was ready for my journey, but before I could leave, I needed to pray for safe travels. I was going to go to the elder's hut to pray, get a night's rest, and would head out in the morning. As I approached the hut, I saw Krozey and some other tribesmen around the same age as me standing around as if they were expecting me. Ever since we were young, if there was trouble to be found Krozey's nose was in it.

"You think you're the Maker's Gift, don't ya?" Krozey said to me.

"What?" I was confused and did not know what he was referring to.

"Let's see it!" another said.

"Yeah, let's see it, pup!" This was followed by a push. "Go into a trance, pup!"

More hands began to shove me.

"You have all gone mad," I said. Why would they try to fight me and force me into a trance? Did they really want to test my power against their own? The elder must have told someone. We lived in a ridiculously small village, and words traveled faster than a Wood Elf rushing to dinner.

Next, I saw a punch come my way. I blocked it with ease and went toe to toe with its thrower.

"I've had enough of this. Shall we, ladies?"

That got their blood going. I readied myself for what they had to give. I tightened my fist and stood my ground. The earth beneath my feet began to tremble. Some of the men's eyes opened wide. They must have felt it, too. Others were too busy running towards me and screaming.

"There will be none of this here!" Zemu spun his staff around and pounded on the heads of a few of the other Foxfang.

"Aw, we were just playing around with the pup."

The elder had a look on his face that said, "I am not buying what you're selling."

"Good thing you did come, Elder. You saved these ladies from a good tussle!" I slapped one's face as a taunt as I followed the elder into his hut.

"Outcast," Krozey said under his breath as he spat on the ground.

"There's always going to be someone who wants to test you," Shadow said to me. I knew exactly what he meant.

"Yes, Father, I know this all too well"

I began to pray. Elder Zemu was looking to feed me to the wolves because maybe he, too, did not believe I could go into a trance. If only they saw what I had saw when the Night Fox entered my body. They would dare not question my abilities. The only thing that bothered me was that I knew that the power was in me; I just had to get it out.

I awoke the next morning with my task on my mind. First, I would have to leave the village and make my way through the woods until I got to the Plains of Pride. From there, it would be at least a four day hike until I met the bottom of the mountains that met the plains. It would be my first time traveling to the mountains, and I planned to learn everything I could from the other people of the world. Whether it be a new potion, a new fight style, or survival skills to keep me alive another day.

"Shall we head out?" A familiar voice shouted out to me. It was Shadow, but I thought I'd be making this journey alone.

"I'm as ready as I'll ever be, Father. Do you know the way there?" "Ah, that's the spirit," he said with a smile on his face. "But you will be on your own when we make it to the Plains of Pride. I have been sought out by Brandon the Brute King. Whatever it may be must be particularly important. He sent a rider from the kingdom, and he reached me late in the night."

We set out after breakfast. I kept thinking that this could be my last home cooked meal. As I left my hut, the eyes of every villager were on me. Most of them did not like me and didn't want me to return. The others wondered why I was traveling alone. And very few wished me luck on my travels, but those who did, I knew they wanted me to return.

Just as I was getting ready to leave the village, a younger Foxfang came up to me and said, "I'm going to be a great adventurer like you someday!"

"What is your name?"

"They call me Zozan."

I shook his hand and smiled.

"Don't be like me, be better." His eyes lit up like stars in a night sky.

Shadow and I continued to walk, and we no longer saw the village or their eyes.

As we entered the wood, the trees blocked the sky; the sunlight had to fight to reach the ground. The forest was cool from the shade and filled with life. All I could think about was reaching the Grey Mountains. I was walking at a pace that seemed like a run, and Shadow was having a hard time keeping up.

"Save your energy, my son. You have a very long way to go, and you're going to need it."

He was right. I was letting my mind get the best of me. I was thinking of getting there and not thinking of what I would actually have to do to make the long journey.

"So, have you gone in a trance on your own yet?"

Him asking that question made it seemed as if he did not believe me.

"No, I have not," I replied with a sigh.

"Well, we are far away enough from the village. You should give it a try."

I stopped walking and looked him in the eye.

"You think so?"

"Sure, what's the worst that can happen?"

I took my stance, tightened my muscles and began to focus my energy.

"AhAAAA!" I cried out. Shadow began to laugh so hard that tears came to his eyes. "Now what is so funny?"

"You, my son. Are you trying to wake every beast in the forest?" He continued to laugh.

"What are you talking about, Father? You asked me to go into a trance."

"Yes, I asked you to go into a trance. I did not ask you to scream your head off like you're going insane. A trance happens when one comes in contact with hidden power, power that you didn't know was there. Once you reach it, it flows through your body, and you will be able to do things you have never imagined. What you were doing was sounding an alarm for every sleeping beast in these woods."

Shadow was right, he was always right. I needed to focus more. Something I was not good at.

"Now, my son, try again."

I closed my eyes, took my stance again, and began to tighten my muscles. I focused on the power I had seen the Night Fox use from within me. I started to cast *fox fire* the same way he did. As I did so, I saw a bright white light in my mind. That was it. That was my hidden power that I needed to come in contact with. I focused on grabbing the light and then casting *fox fire*. The blast was huge, but it was nothing like the one the Night Fox unleashed.

Shadow seem very amazed, but if he would have seen what the Night Fox did, he would have fainted.

"Why the sad face, my son?"

I really did not have the heart to say that was not the best I could do. I felt a little disappointed in myself. I know I should not have, but seeing the Night Fox then looking at the display of power I just did. How could I have not felt that way?

"That was not the best I could do, Father."

"What do you mean?" he replied as if I was out of my mind.

"When the Night Fox entered my body, the blast that came from me was well over the size of that. It was so powerful. It blew a hole through the temple, took down half a mountain, and cleared a forest like it was nothing at all."

Hearing those words, he was more amazed.

"Not only were you able to go into a trance on your first try, my son, but you are telling me that you have more inside you?"

He was absolutely correct. There was much more inside me. This was only a taste, like giving a dog a bone when he knows that you have a whole cow waiting for him. I began to smile.

"Father, that just means I got more training that I need to do."

How much more, I did not know. From the looks of things, it seemed like I needed a lifetime of training to do what the Night Fox did.

As we continued to walk down, there was a carriage on the side of the road.

"Looks like she is in need of aid, Father. Let us give her a hand."

I made haste to try and help her, and Shadow kept the same pace.

As I approached the carriage, I realized the lady in there hit a stump and was ran off the road. From the looks of it, she was pretty banged up from it; bruised on her face, and there was a cut on her cheek. In her hands, she held a child wrapped in cloth. I reached my hand in the carriage to help get her out, and she pulled me in and began to laugh. I was a fool and was played into her trap!

She whistled and shouted out, "We got another one, girls!"

Traveling bandits taking advantage of others kindness is what they were. Two more women dressed in black with masks over their faces jumped out the woods and began to head towards Shadow. He did not seem to intimidated by them at all. Me, on the other hand, I was face-to-face with the woman in the carriage. She was trying to take my gold from me, but I was putting up a fight. The baby that she held in her arms turned out to be a rock, and she bashed it against my head once. That caught me off guard.

These were very sloppy bandits. She lifted the rock above her head to hit me again, but before she could, I pinned one of her wrists to the roof of the carriage with my foot. This made her lose her grip on the rock baby, and it fell on her head. I picked up the baby and smashed the bandit bitch in the face with it. This brought tears to her eyes. She opened the carriage and ran. I darted after her to retrieve my gold.

The two bandit women were closing in on Shadow.

"I'm going to give you one chance to walk away. After that, I will inflict pain on you."

The two women laughed and continued to approach him.

"You, old fool, you think your magic can work on us?"

"No, you young imbecile, I know it can."

Shadow threw his staff on the ground, and they began to laugh at him. One of the girls steadily marched to him; the other did not move.

"Why are you falling behind? This old fool doesn't need his gold!"

"I can't move!" she shouted out. What she did not know was that if Shadow or his staff touched something's shadow, it could not move.

"What kinda spell did you cast on my sister, old man?"

Shadow smiled.

"Oh, you young imbecile, I have not even begun to cast any spells."

"Is name calling all you can do? I'm going to shove those words down your throat!"

"You called me old fool, I called you young imbecile."

She began to charge at him with a short blade. As she was running towards him, she did not realize that he was waiting for her to get closer. As soon as she got close enough, he put his foot on her shadow, and she stopped dead in her tracks.

"What the? What kind of wizard are you?" she demanded.

"I am a shadow wizard, you young imbecile." He laughed and began to stretch her shadow, which made her body look like it was on the rack. Her screams echoed the forest, and her sister watched helplessly.

Hearing her sister scream, the bandit I was chasing pulled a knife from her garter and started slicing madly at the air in my direction.

"Tell the old man to let my sister go, or I'll slice your throat!"

The other bandit watching shouted at the top of her lungs, "Stop! You're going to kill her!"

"I don't plan on killing anyone. She put herself in this position by charging at me. Give us the gold back, and we will go on our way and you can go on yours."

The bandit I was chasing dropped my gold and rushed to her sister. Shadow could have ended their lives, I think he was trying to teach them a lesson.

They did as Shadow asked and returned the gold, and Shadow released their sister.

"Who are you, and why are you holding travelers up for gold on this road?" I asked.

"A girl's got to make a living somehow without selling her body." She winked at me.

She was hesitant to give me her name. "I am Rita the Coin, and we are the Kardwell Sisters." She had not shown any interest in me, but was now being flirtatious. She lightly ran her thumb down my jaw line as she was saying. "If you're ever in Brevell, come see me, so I can repay you for sparing my sister's life."

She blew me a kiss and they went their way and we continued ours.

I had been in these woods and played many times there as a child. I explored every route in and every route out. I even made a few of my own. Traveling with my father, ment sticking to the main road. Which was dangerous, but he did not seem to care. He was incredibly good at defending himself.

"Father, could you have really killed that girl back there?"

He took a few more steps into silence, then he said, "I could have picked them apart before they poked their heads out the woods. I knew they were not killers, just misguided thieves, that is all. You ran in headfirst without checking your surroundings. Be more aware of your surroundings."

I could tell Shadow was trying to make a point. He never treated me like a child; even when I was younger, he talked to me like a man or the man he was raising me to be. I guess that's why I respected him so much. *Everything that's happened, everything we went through in life, there is a lesson to be learned.* He would always say that to me, and I would always learn something new.

It was getting dark; we were coming up on the Elven village of Tree Top Canopy. There were many types of Elves and even more Elven villages. We were going to be staying the night with the Wood Elves of Tree Top Canopy. I had been here few times as a child, and I am sure Shadow had been here countless numbers of times. Shadow became allies with King Ottusleaf VI long ago. He was welcomed with open arms. Anyone a friend of Shadow was a friend of the Tree Top Canopy. This village was full of elf homes that were only in the treetops and were guarded by knight archers. Elves were some of the best archers of the land. In this village, each knight archer was able to stick an arrow in every piece of territory that belonged to them in the blink of an eye. So, if one person were out of line, more than 50 arrows would be coming their way faster than they could draw a sword. Any wrong doer who came along trespassing was either foolish or had a death wish.

The village is one remarkably large tree that supported the whole town. Think of it as if a giant were standing up with arms out, holding up a town that did not touch the ground. For people who were walking, there was only one way into this town. There was a guarded statue of the head of the first king of Tree Top Canopy. When recited the spell in ancient elf tongue, the mouth would open up, and stairs would come out of it. Seeing this as a child made me smile all the time. The elves of the village were incredibly good jumpers and did not need the steps to get from the bottom to the top. They jumped so well that you would think they were flying. Their ability to jump and their marksmanship with arrows made them very deadly with aerial attacks.

As we approached the head of King Ottusleaf, we were welcomed with open arms. Father had arranged that we stay in the palace with

the King. We were just going to eat and get a night's rest and be on our way. I had been in the village, but never in the palace. Pit, I had never even met the king. At this very moment, I was about to do both.

As we made our way to the palace, a few of the locals who knew Shadow welcomed him and shook his hand. I could tell he was tired. Many wanted to talk, but he was polite and kept it short with them. My eyes were so tangled on the surroundings, I barely spoke to anyone. I kept wondering how one tree could have a whole town sitting in it. The houses here were more detailed than our Foxfang huts. The elves even had two or three of them stacked high. We could have learned something from them. The first thing I noticed about the palace was that it was not a castle. It was a smaller tree on top of the bigger one. There were two doors that were carved out of the bark of the tree that held up the town, and they both had the Moon Leaf sigil carved into them.

Four wooden statues blocked us from going in, we had to move around them. As Shadow reached for the door.

"Halt in the name of the King!" the statue cried out. Then it transformed into a living, breathing elf.

We were greeted by four Tree Top Canopy Knights; they were not equipped with bows. These must have been the King's elite guards, two with sword and shield and dressed in ancient elf armor that I had never seen before. The other two knights were dressed in the same armor but had spears.

The door behind them opened, and the King walked towards us. He was dressed in white and green silks held together by silver threads. He walked like a warrior, but his hands had the look that they have not seen battle in a while. Even though he may have not seen battle in some time he still wore his hair proudly in an Elven War-braid.

"Stand down." he ordered his guards, and they did at once. As he got closer, I began to kneel to His Highness. He grinned and said, "No need to kneel; you are amongst friends!" He chuckled. "Shadow, my old friend! How long has it been?" he rejoiced.

"I'm afraid I don't have enough toes or fingers to count the years!"

They both laughed and gave each other a hug.

"You'll have to forgive my guards. We've been under tighter security since our tomb has been tampered with."

"Very interesting," Shadow replied.

"Could it be…?" I tapped Shadow on the arm.

"Could it be what?" King Ottusleaf replied.

"Some bandits have been stealing the bones of the Night Fox Tomb and making weapons out of them. Could the same bandits be tampering with your tomb?"

King Ottusleaf had a puzzled look on his face and agreed with Shadow.

"That is very interesting, but stealing the bones of Wood Elves won't help you to make magic weapons and armors. I believe they are stealing them for a different reason. You see, the bones of the fallen elves are placed in this tree, and the tree uses the magic left in their bones to grow taller and stronger. My goodness—where are my manners? I am Barkley Ottusleaf VI, and you are?"

"I am Zek, first of his name son of D'jzoe." I shook his hand firmly.

"So, it could be the same bandits, but why would they want to weaken the tree?" King Ottusleaf asked himself, but was looking at us.

We followed him into the palace. The floors were made from ivories. There was a green carpet that showed us the way into the giant halls. Straight ahead was a large, open room where the throne set. The walls were covered with paintings of kings of the yesteryears. On both sides of us were stairs that connected at the top and led to the King's personal chambers. Just beyond the stairs were two hallways, one on each side of the room. To the left was the King's kitchen and dining area; to the right was the King's study, lined wall-to-wall with books, maps, and scrolls.

Not many appreciated elf craftsmanship, but I did. I found myself getting lost in thought, feeling the walls, and wondering what it would be like to live in a place like this among the elves. Shadow gave me a nudge to keep up because I was falling behind.

The King led us into the dining area where a feast was already made and waiting for us. There were two large tables on both sides of the room and a smaller table in between those two. The smaller table belonged to the King, because at the head of the table was a chair that had the Moon Leaf sigil on it. The sounds of eleven harps, flutes, and drums filled the room, along with the laughter and cheers of the others. The sweet smell of elvish wines, bread and other delicious items filled the air.

"What's the occasion?" I asked.

"No occasion, just dinner," King Ottusleaf said with a smile.

"I could really get used to this place."

The King's smile got wider and led us to his table.

He led us to the table and introduced us to his family.

"This is my wife, Queen Elnor. My dear, you remember Master Shadow? And this is his grandson, Zek."

"How could I forget? He comes to your aid more than any of your cousins. He has saved your hide from a tanning one too many times. I often question if something is going on between you two."

Shadow had very dark skin, but somehow she still made him blush.

"My lady, it is always an honor to see you," he kissed her hand and bowed his head.

"These are the twins Alwin and Elwin. You will have to excuse them they seem to share one brain. And the future Queen of Tree Top Canopy, Elra."

He picked his daughter up and swung her around. She giggled as he twirled her. She could not have been more than six years of age.

"A lovely family you have, Your Highness."

"How come you have fuzzy ears, and your grandfather doesn't?" Elra asked.

The twins laughed at their younger sister's harmless rudeness, but the queen snapped at her.

"Elra! Don't be rude to our guest!"

"It's quite alright, my Queen. I will be glad to explain. Elra, I am a Foxfang. We are part man, part fox. We too live in houses high in the trees, but not nearly as nice as the ones here. My grandfather, Shadow, raised me since I was a pup. He taught me everything. He's not blood to me, but loyalty makes us closer."

Elra nodded her head.

"So, you're an orphan?"

The whole table laughed, everyone except Queen Elnor. She slammed her palm on the table, and the laughs stopped.

"No, I'm not an orphan. I have a family, but Shadow raised me."

The twins still had grins on their faces, but their mother had a look that said, "stop," and they turned the other way.

"Let us eat," King Ottusleaf said.

The food was delicious; every bite was like a taste of divine. Plates of potatoes, bowls of fruit, plates of salads and breads. Everything but meat. There were many different types of wines, but I did not overindulge.

Over at the next table, I heard some men betting—about what, I did not know. There were many of them crowded around. I tapped Alwin.

"What is it that they are wagering on?" I asked.

"Race through the woods," both twins replied.

"Doesn't seem too bad. Why wager?"

"Speed is everything," said Alwin.

"Yeah, speed is everything!" Elwin echoed. "Let us show you, Foxfang. Father, may we be excused?"

They both seemed very eager about this. The King gave a nod, and we headed over to a door at the end of the dining area that led to the outside. Bugs of the night lit the sky. We were high above the trees; I did not understand where they were racing to.

"So, what is it that they wager?" I asked.

"You see that stone right there?" Alwin pointed.

"Yeah, that stone?" Elwin echoed. "Well, the loser has to strap it to their back, and they are wagering how many times they will climb up and down the tree."

My eyes nearly popped out of my head. This rock was huge; I am not even sure how they got it into the tree. On top of that, to climb the tree with it on their backs! The elves had a funny way to entertain themselves. None of them looked like they could pick it up, but they were wagering many times. Some wagered four others, but others, nines, and tens.

"Well, a race doesn't seem to be too hard," I said.

The crowd got silent for a moment, then they began to laugh.

One man in the crowd patted me on the back and said, "If it's not so hard, you're up next."

"Yeah!" The crowd roared and pushed me to the start.

I smiled. "And who wishes to challenge me?"

"Ooooo!" the crowd said. Many of them laughed. "Krinkels!" they all shouted.

"Yeah, Krinkels!" the twins echoed.

"You wana race?" Krinkels said with his hand out like he was going to receive something from me. "How much do you wager?" he asked.

I sat my sack of gold on the table, and they all laughed once again. Krinkels walked over to me and placed his hand on my shoulder.

"My friend, you must have not been in the treetops for long. Gold is no good up here." He walked over to the rock and placed his hand on it. "This!" he smacked the rock. "This is what we wager." He picked up the rock and then threw it on his back and began squatting it.

The crowd began to cheer.

"Oh yes, that feels good." he said. "What's your name friend?"

"The name is Zek of the Foxfang."

"Well, Zek, my Foxfang friend. How much should we wager?"

The crowd shouted out numbers.

"Six. How about we wager six of them," I said.

"Six?" Krinkels asked. "Six it is."

The crowd cheered. Their roars filled the dining area. They were so loud that the King and Shadow got out of their seats to come see what was going to happen.

"But wait—I don't know the course."

The twins came over and stroked my shoulders.

"Just follow the branch."

"Yes, the branch!"

"You mean to tell me the whole race takes place on one branch?"

"Do you have muck in your ears? That's what I said, isn't it?"

"Yeah, what he said."

The King was right beside me and he began to smile. He lifted his hand and said, "Ready?"

Krinkels and I took our starting stance and nodded at each other.

"GO!" The King shouted and the crowd lit up with excitement.

We bolted when we heard the King's command. I gave it my all, and somehow, I was in the lead. The branch we were on was very thick. I was running like I had a dragon hot on my heels. The branch went straight and then started to slant down. I knew the race could not have been that hard. After the slant, there was a sharp left and then another left followed by a slant down to the right. After the slant to the right, I lost my footing and nearly fell off the branch. My nails dug deep into the branch's bark.

At this moment, I realized Krinkels was holding back the whole time. He caught up to me.

"See you at the finish, my friend."

I am terrified of heights. I looked down; we were up so high. I could not even see the ground. The bugs of the moonlight and the torches that everyone was holding at the start were the only lights I could see. I was going to have to get it together if I wanted to best Krinkels in a foot race.

I swung myself back on to the tree and took off after him. The only thing I could think about is how much I did not want to have a boulder tied to my back and have to climb up and down a tree that you could not even see the ground from the top of it. The branch went on straight for a way, but it was not smooth. This part of the branch was covered in vines and smaller branches. Finding footing was a must. I could see Krinkels running along the branch as if he already knew where to place his feet. I was gaining on him, but I was also trying to be as careful as I could so that I did not find myself taking tumble.

The branch began to slant up and had notches in it as if someone had taken an ax to it to make steps that led up. Krinkels was somehow able to climb this part without using his hands. He was jumping, skipping three to four steps at a time. My legs started to grow weak after the third time I tried to follow his method. I started using my arms to hurl myself higher and higher. This worked out better for me and brought me closer to his heels. The eyes of people in their homes began to meet mine. I could hear cheers from them. I was not sure if they were cheering for me or Krinkels. I could see the steps coming to an end, and I was almost caught up to Krinkels. My hands were landing right next to his feet each step that he took.

Just as we came to the end of the steps, my hand was stepped on by Krinkels. I am guessing it was an accident because his face turned a shade lighter as if he was horrified. Me, being in pain and not wanting to show anger, dug my nails deep into the wood steps and hurled myself in front of him. I dug so deep that I took a chunk of wood off the steps.

We were neck and neck when the steps ended, and the branch began to spiral down. I was amazed that we were still on the same branch. It was like someone crafted this tree themselves. From the top of the spiraled wood, I could see everyone's torches. We were getting closer to the finish. We were running downhill, gaining more and more speed, making it harder to control our feet. Krinkels leaped into the air and then began to slide the rest of the way down the spiraled wood. This put him ahead of me quite a ways. I leaped into the air and landed myself right beside him and kept running.

The spiral ended, and we were at the last stretch. Everyone at the finish roared for Krinkels, only Shadow and a few others cheered for me. I was giving it my all, but at this point I could not tell if Krinkels was playing with me or not…

He was. Just as I thought that I had him, he leaped in the air once again and landed himself at the finish. As I crossed the finish line, everyone patted me on the back and told me how good of a show I put on for them. Krinkels did not seem to be too winded, but I on the other hand could hardly stand up straight let alone get a word out.

Krinkels came to me and shook my hand.

"That was the closest anyone came to beating me!" he smiled. I guessed he likes to run.

Shadow patted me on the back, and the King shook my hand as well.

"You must have a lot of faith in yourself to race the fastest elf in the woods."

"Yes! The fastest in the woods," the twins echoed behind their father.

I was shocked and very surprised to hear him say that. If I would have known he was the fastest elf in the woods, I probably would not have raced him. I also really did not even have a say in the matter. I guess me giving the fastest elf in the woods his first loss would have made more of the elves respect me, but almost besting him made them like me just a little bit more.

"How was I supposed to know Krinkels was the fastest in the woods?"

Shadow looked at me and smiled.

"By being aware of your surroundings."

I could not figure out what he meant; my mind was drawing a blank. Then it hit me. No one else was racing him, and his was the first name that they shouted. I fed myself to the wolves this time.

"Ahh," I said to Shadow, and we both laughed for a moment, for yet another lesson was learned here.

"Alright, everyone, that's enough races for one night." The King said in a calm but very stern voice. Some of the elves went to their homes; the others went back to their seats and finished their meals.

"I'm off to bed, my son. Do not stay out too long; we have to be up with the birds." Shadow yawned and walked to the guest chambers the king had prepared for us.

Krinkels and I sat and talked a while longer. He gave me pointers and instructed me on ways to move faster through the woods.

"Next time you are in the treetops, I'll have to show you how we get so fast."

"Sounds like a grand idea. I am headed to the Grey Mountains at sunrise. When I return from my journey I shall seek you out.."

"The Grey Mountains, you say. Sounds like quite the journey you have ahead of you. I will not bend your ear any longer. When you return, make sure you seek me out."

"Will do, Krinkels. See you when I return."

"Safe travels, Zek."

I stretched myself out and set off to bed.

"Oh, but before you go: You still owe the tree six stones."

Krinkels and I shared a laugh for a moment. He helped me strap the rock to my back, and he went off to bed. I took my first step climbing down the tree and realized it was going to be a long night. Did I mention I was terrified of heights?

The sun was just about to rise, and I was on my last stone. Shadow was already awake and enjoying his morning ritual. After the third time up the tree, my muscles were not sore. My bones were. I felt as if the stone was a part of me, and I realized that doing this every day as a child must have been the way they were able to move the way that they did.

As I reached the top of the tree after doing my last stone, Krinkels and a few others from last night were there to congratulate me.

"Let me help you with this burden. You know, they took bets on you. Many thought that you would not make it." He pointed behind him, and a group of elves were getting stones tied to their backs.

I laughed, "You do not have faith in your Foxfang friend?"

The few who were getting the stones on them shooed me away and grunted. The others laughed; seeing their wagers being paid off in stones made them happy.

"Not many outsiders can finish their set of stones. I am glad you proved them wrong. I myself am ashamed that I doubted you also."

"Then why aren't you getting strapped in?"

"I doubted you. I did not wager on you."

Krinkels shook my hand, and I met up with Shadow. He was saying his farewells to the King. The King, too, congratulated me on my success of completing my stones. We made our way down the steps to continue our way.

"Quite a night you had last night, my son," Shadow said softly. "Yes, a lesson was learned, and I made a few new friends. Krinkels offered to teach me the way of the wood when I return from the Grey Mountains. He's going to show me how to move about the same way the Wood Elves do in the canopies."

I jumped up in the air; I was lighter on my feet than I had ever been. It would have seemed that I was floating. As I landed on the ground, I took another leap into the air. This time I scaled up a tree.

"All of this, I was able to learn from one night of doing stones," I shouted from the top of the tree and took a bow. Shadow was impressed and applauded me.

Then, Shadow's face became serious. He sensed something out in the distance.

I fixed my eyes in the direction he was looking to see if I could catch a glimpse.

"I know those flames," he whispered under his breath. Shadow took the form of tree shadows and made his way over to the glowing brightness in the distance.

I hopped from treetop to treetop to try and keep up with him, but I could not. He was moving too fast. At the edge of the forest, he sat in the last tree's shadow and looked over the situation. I was still a ways behind him, and I still could not fully see what was going on.

When i got to the tree where Shadow had been, he had already acted.

He put up a shadow barrier and trapped himself inside with the flames. Some of the flames outside the barrier were dancing along the grass and moving towards the forest. The trees started to move. The flames woke the Treefolk, and they began to move as fast as they could back deeper into the woods from the flames. I could hear the clashing of swords and yelling, but I could not see inside the barrier. I drew my sword and ran into the barrier, but came out on the other side.

There was no way I could get into there to help Shadow or see what was happening.

The sound of fighting went on for a few more moments and then the barrier faded. There were five burnt bodies on the ground, and their bodies were smoking as if their flames where just being put out. Shadow was holding a young man with flames for hair in his arms. The Elder of the Treefolk, Oaklock Longroot, picked up a large pile of dirt and put the rest of the flames out.

"Master Shadow, what a surprise to see you here," Oaklock said slowly and in a very deep voice that you could feel in your chest. "Elder Longroot, we were just passing through, and I saw the flames. I rushed as fast as I could to put them out. I apologize; did not mean to wake your kin."

"No need for an apology, my friend. I watched the whole tussle with my own eyes. Is the boy alright?"

"He is fine, still breathing. Just a little roughed up, that's all." The young man was coming to; he opened his eyes and stood up. "Thank you," the young man said, trying to keep his balance and stand on his own. Shadow acted as if he knew the man for a long time. Oaklock took a good look at the man's face.

"Looks like we are in the presence of royalty."

Oaklock and the other treefolk took a bow. The young man fainted, and Shadow rushed over to him.

It was Heat Scorchis II, the Prince of Flames, the bloodline of the Creator of Flames. Royalty was right; his father, Heat was the King of Flames. He was able to control any kind of flame there was. Shadow told me stories of how he would make large dragons out of the flame from a candle, or if a field was on fire, he could make all the flames

disappear. If someone was to cast a *fire ball* spell, he could make it grow bigger than you could ever imagine. His son was here in front of us.

"His presence here troubles me," Shadow scratched his head.

"You are right. The Prince of Flames being this far away from home… What could this mean?" Oaklock seemed very wise and knew whatever Heat Jr. was doing here could not have meant anything good. We sat around waiting for Heat Jr. to regain consciousness. I only heard stories from Shadow; I had never met or heard anyone else speak of the Scorchis. Oaklock seemed to know a lot about his father, telling stories of how he was saved by Heat's father and how he witnessed Heat whipping out armies in a blink of an eye. Or putting out the flames to a sea of fire. The stories made them seem like very violent people, but Shadow says that they only would use their powers for good.

"I'll kill them all," Heat Jr. shouted, and the flames on his head flared up like someone threw oil on a fire as he came to. He must have been having a nightmare or remembered he was in a heated battle.

"Are you alright? Who were those men? Why were they after you?" Shadow was full of questions.

"Shadow, I am fine. We must leave now," Heat Jr. did not notice himself yelling and must have not known we could hear him clearly. "Those men were traitors! They killed my father! They were his Elite Guards. They did not agree with waiting to go to war, so they waited until he went to sleep and slaughtered him in his sleep. We must leave now!"

Shadow was silent for a moment.

"A flame could never die." he whispered. There was a bit of a silence between them.

"A flame can never die" Heat Jr. repeated. I did not understand what they spoke of; I did not want to ask any questions. If my father would have just been killed, I would not be in the mood to answer any questions. I stayed silent as Heat Jr. went into more details about the mutiny that took place at his castle.

Shadow was silent for a moment. His longtime ally was dead, and his homeland was facing a civil war.

"Heat, I would really like to help you, but I must speak to the King of Brevell Brandon; he has summoned me." Shadow paused for a moment; the way he spoke, I could tell he really wanted to help Heat

Jr. "I will send my grandson, Zek, with you in my place."

My eyes became wide. Why would Shadow volunteer me to go fight in a civil war in a land where I know nothing about? I kept silent and nodded my head.

"As soon as I get to the Kingdom of Brevell, I will have the king send troops to aid you until I can make my way there." The way Shadow spoke made it seem like it pained him not to be able to help his ally.

"Thank you, Master Shadow. It's an honor to finally meet you, and you grace me by helping." Heat Jr. seemed to be fine with the fact of me stepping in for Shadow.

"But," Shadow added, "when you finish taking back your homeland, you must aid Zek, and put an end to the bandits who disgrace his ancestors' tomb."

The flames on Heat Jr.'s head began to rise.

"What kind of monsters would do such a thing? Life is already hard. Can you not get peace and death either?" Heat Jr. put his right fist on his chest and shouted, "Any man who would aid me in my time of need

45

is an ally and a lifelong friend." He extended a hand out for me to shake. "From this day forth, we will be Brothers of the Flame."

As I shook his hand, he brought his other arm around for a hug. I thought it to be a little too much as a ritual, but from where he is from, I am guessing this is necessary. From this day forward, we would be Brothers of the Flame; this meant that our swords would fight for one another, and our shields would shield one another. I did not have a problem with this; it's not every day you meet the Prince of Flames. He chose to make me an ally. I was going to be crossing swords with grave robbing bandits; I could use all the help I could get.

Shadow said his farewells and headed for the Kingdom of Brevell. I did not know how long it would be until I would see him again, or if I would ever see him again. I know Shadow would be alright; it was me that I was worried about. The lack of details the Night Fox gave me was a bit haunting. I was to travel to a faraway place I had never been and stop a group of people I did not know their numbers, their abilities, or their background. It almost seemed like hunting a wild boar on a pitch-dark night.

As Shadow walked away in the distance, I waited with Heat Jr. until he had enough strength to make his way back to his homeland. I myself was tired from doing the stones from last night. Not getting a wink of shuteye, but I had the will to push on and to put an end to the madness at the Night Fox Tomb. I was very sleepy, I knew that if I slept now, there would be no waking me. I kept myself awake by talking to Heat Jr.

"So, what is your homeland like?" I asked.

Heat Jr. sat silently as if I struck a nerve.

"Zek, how far have you traveled from your village?"

"Not very," I replied. I am not sure what that had to do with the question I asked him.

"Outside the forest life is very different. Here your people care about one another. Out there... Maybe every now and again you will find a kind hearted soul like you or myself who cares about others, but other than that. Every man for himself, one man on top one man on bottom, or outdo the next man. That is usually how people see life. My people were known for being peaceful but well known for our short tempers. I live in a castle deep in the mountains. The castle its self is a fortress, and the peaks of the mountains that surround us makes it even harder for enemy forces to attack. Four massive, square towers surround the castle; they reach twice the height of the walls and are connected by large, thick walls made of light red stone. A huge gate with massive metal doors and hot oil pots gives us a safe place in our mountain stronghold. At night, the towers are home to the flames that burn so bright, it makes it seem like the sun is shining. It's not the prettiest of castles, but it's home."

The description Heat Jr. had given me made it seem like he lived in a lifeless place; I could tell he was trying to talk it down. For some reason, his homeland excited me.

After sitting around talking one another ear off, we were finally going to make our way to Heat Jr.'s castle. We would have to cross the plains and that would bring us to the foot of the Grey Mountains.

"It's going to be about a three day walk," Heat Jr. said with a smile on his face.

"I'm aware of that."

"We need to make haste. How are your sword handling skills?"

"My skills can't be taught," I laughed, they were good going up against the people in my village. I wasn't too sure how they would match up against Heat Jr.

"Well, I'm glad to hear you say that. We are going to take a detour to the fighting pits."

"I've never been to the fighting pits. My people don't believe in fighting to make a profit," I explained to Heat Jr., but he already had his mind set on us going.

"We're just going to make enough coin to buy us two horses and then be on our way."

That sounded reasonable. Traveling by horseback would surely get us to our destination faster, but it would be one day of traveling on the Dansdill Road in a different direction. We would be crossing the sands, not the plains. The fighting pits rested close to where the desert met the plains. We did not have to worry too much about bandits because the area was mostly flat, and we could see anyone coming towards us far as the eye could see.

You could become a wealthy man in the fighting pits. If you were a fighter or just making bets, the fighting pits would have you as long if you had the coin to back it up. The Dansdill Road housed traveling merchants that came to and from the fighting pits trying to sell their wares. Merchants who were coming from the fighting pits usually had the weapons and armor of the fighters who lost in the pits. The selling of a defeated fighters' armor, to me, seemed a bit grotesque, but Heat Jr. kept telling me it was just a way of life for some people. Everyone in the fighting pits had an important role to play, from the collectors of the bets, to the fighters, to merchants, and even the people who cleaned up the blood. Everyone did their part, and everyone got paid; this has been going on for generations, and everyone was happy. It all just seemed wrong; deep down inside, I knew he was right. If they did not want to clean blood, they did not have to; if they did not want to fight, they did not have to. He was right.

"Is there anywhere to get a good meal around here?" I asked Heat Jr. with my belly rumbling like a dog who had not eaten in weeks.

"There are meat and fruit stands all around us," Heat Jr. replied, "but if you want a real hot meal and a place to rest there is an inn about half way on the road called Crimson Star Inn."

I could either spend what little coins I had left on fruits and sundried rodents, or wait it out until we got to the inn. I glanced over at a merchant cart and saw some of his sundried meats; they did not look like they would fill the tiniest hole in my stomach.

As we continued our walk, we began to see more and more merchants. There were buyers and collectors of armor at every booth. I was surprised to see so many different armors and weapons from around the world. People came from all over to try their luck in the pits. Up in the distance, we heard a merchant shouting noticeably louder than the others around him selling his wares.

"Ever wanted to go to the Blukx Marshlands, but never had the coin to travel? Well, no need to fret! I have brought the Blukx Marshlands, and its wares to you. The Eagar Crow has what you need from bows to long swords and boots to helms."

I had never been to the marshlands, but I had met a few people from there. They say it is one of the hardest places to live, given the extreme difference in weather.

"Zek! We must check out his inventory!" Heat Jr. exclaimed.

When we approached the merchant, the first thing I noticed that everything he had was nothing like I had ever seen before. Everything was exotic. I see now why Heat Jr. wanted to see his wares.

"The name is Ivan the Lucky. What can I help you young lords with?" He introduced himself as if he knew what we were up to. He looked to be a very healthy man, not fat and able to hold his own. Even though he has a wooden hand.

"We are just passing through," I explained to Ivan.

Heat Jr. had his eyes fixed on what Ivan had for sale.

"You seem to be quite a ways from home, my Lord," He directed this statement at Heat Jr. "Do not worry. Your secret's safe with me. I am not here to start trouble. I am just here to make coin. Being a traveling merchant, you see lots of things and go many of places." Ivan the Lucky must have seen Heat Jr. people before; how else would he have known that he was a Lord?

Heat Jr. nodded his head and continued shopping.

"Anything in particular I can help you with?"

"Well, we are going to the fighting pits. Maybe you have something that would help me not stand out like an albino slave monkey." Heat Jr. winked and pointed at his flames.

Ivan turned around and opened a trunk.

"Try this on." He handed Heat Jr. a leather Helm with squared opening leaving just the eyes exposed. Attached to the top was a thick layer of exotic animal fur, covering every surface.

"No, I think my flames might get the best of this one." Heat Jr. handed it back, and Ivan turned around to search again.

This time, Ivan pulled out a mask of a creature's face that I had never laid eyes on before. The face was faded black with a silver lining around the eyes and the mouth. The mask gave off a look that seemed lifeless and had half a smile on it. It covered Heat Jr.'s flames and his face, so no one would know who he was.

Heat Jr. tried on the mask, and it fit perfectly.

"Ahh, I knew you would like this one. It is called the Crown of Nightmares. It belonged to a battle mage from Gem Cove, but I managed to get my hand on it," Ivan laughed and nudged Heat Jr. with his wooden hand making a wise banter. I found it a bit humorous, but I do believe Heat Jr. got the biggest kick out of it.

"How much for the crown?" Heat Jr. asked.

"I'm going to put this one on the house. Let's call this my good deed of the day."

Ivan handed Heat Jr. the mask and did not charge him any gold at all.

"Where you two heading?" Ivan asked.

"We are headed to the Crimson Star to fill our bellies."

"I'm a bit hungry myself. How about I give you a ride?"

Heat Jr. and I nodded and agreed. Ivan packed up his horse and his wares and gave us a ride to the Crimson Star Inn.

Ivan giving us a ride gave us a little more daylight to travel. We got to the inn; Ivan tied up his horse, and Heat Jr. and I walked inside. The inside looked better than the outside. There was a large bar with three barrels of ale behind it. There was a large fireplace and walls that were cherry oak and covered with paintings and rugs with different styles of stars on them. We found ourselves a table in the corner and had a seat.

Ivan yelled across the room to the innkeeper.

"A bowl of your chowder and one hen for each of my friends." The innkeeper nodded and had a maid make it up for us. "So, what brings ya lads this way?"

Heat Jr. and I looked at each other and replied, "Family business," which was true.

"Well, I won't keep ya long. Just feed you and send you on your way. Maybe the Maker will send some luck my way," Ivan said.

"Why is it that they call you Ivan the Lucky?" Heat Jr. asked.

"'Cus I'm lucky they only took the hand, not me arm," he yelled, lifting his wooden hand. Our table was full of laughter; we ate with a stranger, and he turned out to be a nice old peddler. He had a story or two for everything.

After we ate, we shook Ivan's hand and thanked him for his generosity. He sent us on our way.

"We still have less than half of a day of traveling to go. If we keep this pace, we can make it to the pits and not have to sleep on the road." Heat Jr. said.

We were getting closer to the fighting pits, there were more vendors, and the crowds of people were growing thicker, and their lies were getting louder. Nightfall was upon us, but the sky was lit up by torches. When we got to the fighting pits, the only thing there was stone steps for sitting and a dirt pit for fighting. It was nothing fancy like the Arena of Bevell. This place was a pit.

"Welcome to Dagger Tip Fighting Pits!" Heat Jr. belted out sarcastically.

"Why do they call it 'Dagger Tip'? Do people actually die?" I asked.

"No, there hasn't been a fight to the death here in over 100 years. The name comes from, whoever stuck their dagger in their opponent first wins." Heat Jr. cheered out. "Let's find us a room before it gets too late; we could sleep with the other fighters, but we're not really fighters, are we?" Heat Jr. made a joke of us not being good enough to be here.

I followed him around from inn to inn, looking for a resting place for the night, but they were all full for the night. No one anywhere had a room for us to rent. If Heat Jr. was not wearing his mask, people would be cleaning rooms themselves to get him a room.

"Looks like we'll be sleeping under the stars tonight, my friend."

We made our way outside and found a piece of dirt to make ours. Heat Jr. lit a fire as I gathered wood. Funny right? We got comfy under the stars and laid down.

"Get a good night rest. I am sure we both going to need it for in the morning," Heat Jr. said.

He was right; after spending a whole night doing stones, then walking all the way here, I figured I was ready—we were both due for a good night's rest.

"What're the fighting pits like?" I asked.

"Think of it, as you remember when you were younger and the older boy would always pick on you? Think of you growing older and smashing his face for each time he pushed you in the mud, smacked you, or took something that belonged to you."

Either Heat Jr. got picked on a lot as a child, or this was where he came to take anger out. I could not tell just yet.

As the sun came up, Heat Jr. was already planning out our day for us. All we needed was 50 silvers, and we could buy ourselves a horse.

"We will be fighting as a pair, so that means more coins for us when we win."

Our first fight would be after breakfast. We would be facing twin elven knights from Ubarst Woodlands. They both used spears and specialized in ranged attacks. Heat Jr. was telling me the best way to go about fighting these two. His plan was to get close to them and mess up their rhythm.

Heat Jr. gave me a nudge and pointed to a man. He told me that man is Logan the Smile, and runs all the bets. He seemed to be a respectable man who looked like he was done fighting in the pits, because of the way he dressed. He wore a dark blue overcoat. It had shiny metal buttons that looked like large coins. It was buttoned all the way to the neck and left it open around the waist area. He wore two throwing knives on each side. I got the message 'I am not a fighter, but I will kill you' from the way he wore his knives. Heat Jr. also told me Logan and his men worked for the Pit Master. Someone who was always watching but never really seen. There was no fancy introducing. We got in the pit, and Logan said, "Fight!"

It had begun.

The twins approached us, and they marched tall in their shiny elf-crafted armor. Spear in one hand, shield in another. The elves towered over us. They had spears that seem to stand nearly two times the length of the elves. They stopped and paused for a moment and then took their fighting stance, shields up to their face and spear facing their target.

"Let's see what you got, Foxfang," Heat Jr. said. He gave me a pat on the back and sent me deeper into the pit. I drew my sword to put an end to these two quickly. Heat Jr. drew his blade, but did not charge into combat. I thought myself fully capable of handling them myself, since we were not killing one another. I stepped left, and my foot was nearly taken off by one of their spears. I stepped left again; this time when he put his spear down, my sword was there to meet it. I stepped right, but this time, when my sword met his spear, the spear went flying. His brother threw him the shield as he went to go get the spear. So now one brother had both shields, and the other had both of their spears. It was amazing to know that they trained with one having both spears and the other both shields. That was unheard of in my part of the woods. They stood close to each other making it so that I was at a distance.

When I got close, I could not do anything because the other was blocking all around them with both shields.

"Has our furry friend met his match?" Logan shouted. The crowd cheered and roared for us to take each other out. I was surprised they did not tell Heat Jr. to fight. I must have been putting on quite the show for them. I circled around them slowly, locking eyes with both of them and trying to listen to the patterns of their feet as they tried to keep up. I slowly began to pick up more speed while circling them to see if they were able to keep up. They were, but just barely.

"Stop dancing!" the crowd booed.

They were right; if I was going to finish this, I was going to have to be quicker than them.

I kept circling. By this time, I was full on running. I planted my left foot and jumped the opposite way I was circling them. They were not ready for that. I found my opening, ran and tackled both of them, knocking both of them off their feet. The crowd of onlookers got even louder. The pit floors rumbled with excitement. The skies were full of echoing voices and hands swaying about.

The twins stood up, reequipped themselves, and smiled. Heat Jr. finally stepped in with his sword drawn. The twins both stood with their weapons pointed at Heat Jr. Both of the knights swung at him he ducked and dodged both of them. They swung again, and he broke both of their spears with his sword. They threw the remaining parts of their spears at Heat Jr. He dodged them both. They threw their shields down and switched to hand-to-hand combat. Heat Jr. ran to the first one, kicked the inside of his thigh to make him lose his footing. Then punched him in his face, sending him to the ground violently. The other swung a heavy punch towards Heat Jr., but it missed by a longshot. Heat Jr. jumped back so gracefully, it looked like he was floating like a fairy. Then Heat Jr.'s answer to the missed punch was a mule kick to the face, sending him to the ground. The crowd roared and stood to their feet as our first fight came to an end.

We took a short breather and watched two more fights. Our second fight was going to start right after. We were to be going against an ax touting warrior from Winter Peak. He requested taking us both on at the same time, which meant more gold for him if he won. He did not seem to be very fast, but I could smell a lot of magic coming from this man. He was not much taller than me, but there was much more to him. It seemed like three of my arms would make one of his. He wore the head of a large horned beast. The fur greaves and boots he wore; I am guessing came from the same creature. The rest of his body was dressed in scars, each one having their own story.

As before, the word "fight" was spoken, and we began. This time I made the first move instead of Heat Jr. pushing me into the battle.

"Be careful out there, Zek," Heat Jr. said. I grinned and continued to walk forward. The Winter Peak warrior swung his ax in a downward motion as if he were trying to squash my head like a melon. I stepped left to dodge it, but as soon as his ax hit the ground, he swung for my head again. I drew my sword; next time he swung his ax, I was going to attempt to block it. He swung at me again. I did not have time to block it with my sword, as he finished his swing, he let the ax go and sent it flying in Heat Jr.'s direction. The crowd shouted; this was the action they wanted to see. Heat Jr. moved, but still did not participate in the fight. I sighed, gripped my sword tighter, and charged the ax warrior. My shoulder thrusted into his chest, knocking him off his feet and closer to his weapon. He picked up his weapon and stared down Heat Jr.. He slowly started walking towards Heat Jr.. I rushed him for another shoulder thrust. He answered with an open hand to my face, pushing me backwards. He had so much power behind it, it seemed like he could have broken my neck. Heat Jr. still did not move; he was taunting the ax warrior. I swung my sword, and he blocked with his ax. He was growing tired of Heat Jr.'s insults. Finally, Heat Jr. drew his sword. The two were going back and forth with blows. The ax hitting the sword made a very loud ear ringing, clashing sound. The ax man swung low, and Heat Jr. jumped on his ax, sticking the ax blade into the ground. Heat Jr. then landed a punch to his face which made him stumble back a few steps. This angered the ax warrior. He threw his ax at me and then charged over to Heat Jr.. The ax warrior began swinging at his face wildly, and threw him against the wall. I managed to deflect the ax and sent it into the crowd of people. Heat Jr. stood up with sword in hand, and I backed the ax warrior against the wall, and the round was over. He did not even use his magic.

Our last round was against the Fencing Ace, Agrippa, and his son. Fencing was swordplay from across the water, which I did not know much about. Heat Jr. did not seem to know too much either. It was still early in the day, and after the fight, we did not get to catch our breath. Heat Jr. did not seem to break a sweat, but I was starting to after dodging those heavy ax attacks. We stood in the pit waiting for our challengers to arrive. When they entered, the crowd of people stood on their feet and roared. The pair of fighters did not look like much of a threat. They were dressed in white padded clothes that looked like they did not offer very much protection. Their swords were not much better. They had a thin piece of triangle shaped metal no thicker than your thumb for a blade. Even with a very sharp tip, it did not seem like it could put a hole in any armor. It also had a large bell-shaped guard to protect the hand and forearm.

The word "fight" was spoken, and the match began. I stepped out forward once again, and Heat Jr. stood back. Agrippa sent his son out; he could not have been more than 10 years of age. He drew his letter opener, and I drew my sword, and we began to dance.

We circled around each other. He looked relaxed; too relaxed. I swung towards him; he parried out the way and swung towards me swinging twice and landing one of the hits on my back. The child smiled at me and went back into his fighting position. He swung at me again; this time he just stood still and was just moving his arm. I managed to dodge all of his hits. I swung at him. He bent his knees, lifted his arm and then landed his sword under my armpit and said, "Fatal hit."

The crowd cheered on the young boy as he made me look like a fool. The boy walked over to his father.

"How about we make this interesting?" Agrippa said.

"What do you have in mind?" Heat Jr. asked.

"How bout we wager one silver for each fatal hit? Whoever gets ten fatal hits first wins. "

I looked over at Heat Jr.. He stood silent for a moment. Unfolded his arms and then said, "You got yourself a deal."

Agrippa's son stepped out of the pit.

Heat Jr. and I laughed.

"He can't be serious, both of us... with the just a pig sticker? And... you must be... we don't have." I whispered to Heat Jr.

"He doesn't know that. Let us make this quick so we can be on our way," Heat Jr. snapped.

We circled around Agrippa. His feet seemed light and would not stop moving. Heat Jr. made the first move by swinging high; Agrippa blocked high. Heat Jr. swung to the left; Agrippa blocked left, with his feet still moving. Heat Jr. swung down low, and Agrippa jumped to dodge it, but when he landed, Heat Jr. had positioned himself behind him and had his blade pointed at his back.

"Fatal hit," Heat Jr. said.

Agrippa smiled and took his fighting stance again. His feet still moving, and him and Heat Jr. continued to circle each other. Heat Jr. began to attack this time. Agrippa blocked it and went on the offensive. He swung at Heat Jr. repeatedly up high in a wild pattern, took a step back, and lunged forward.

"Fatal and fatal," Agrippa said with a smile. He had placed two well-placed nicks on Heat Jr.'s neck, drawing blood. Both would have been fatal if this were a fight to the death. The crowd went wild with cheer. The two stared each other down. This time, Heat Jr. found himself defending himself from Agrippa's attack. Agrippa was no doubt a well-trained swordsman. This is the most action I have seen from Heat Jr. all day. Agrippa seemed very relaxed while fighting, and very arrogant, but he was not. He was just a good swords master. Agrippa took a step back; Heat Jr. swung, and Agrippa lunged forward under Heat Jr. and placed a fatal hit under Heat Jr.'s armpit. The crowd was on their feet cheering.

Agrippa motioned me over to him. As I walked over, he took his fighting stance. He took a step forward swinging up high; I blocked, and he spun around behind me and swatted me on my backside with his sword. The crowd laughed. I took a step back, and Agrippa returned to his fighting stance. This time he began his attack down low and worked his way up. I blocked him every time. He hit my left inner thigh and my right inner thigh and then my left again; took a step back and lunged forward again, this time his weapon landed on my manhood.

"Fatal hit?" he asked sarcastically. The crowd laughed again. I took my fighting stance as he took his. He began to attack me, but this time, I attacked faster and more aggressively. I was backing him into the corner. When I got close enough, I jumped and placed my foot on the wall; this landed me behind him. I kneed him in the back and sent him to the ground. He landed on his stomach, and before he could get up,

I placed my sword on the back of his neck.

"Fatal hit."

"So, it would seem you know how to take down an opponent, let us finish this once and for all," Aggripa said. He motioned Heat Jr. over; he was going to take the two of us on by himself. He took his fighting stance, and Heat Jr. charged in. Heat Jr. swung, but Agrippa blocked everything that came his way. I jumped in behind Heat Jr., Agrippa took a step back and lunged towards me. I managed to deflect it. If it would had landed, it would have been a fatal hit. I could not believe he was taking the both of us on blocking and dodging everything we sent his way. He had been playing with us the whole time. The more Agrippa danced around us, the more Heat Jr. grew angry.

So far Heat Jr. and I each only got one fatal hit on Agrippa. We both truly underestimated his skills. He somehow knew how to lead us on and open ourselves up for his attacks. We owed him six coins at this point. If this kept up, we would not have enough coins to buy the horses. That would also mean we would have to enter in another fight, which would set us back in our journey to the Grey Mountains. It was time we fought wiser, which was hard. Only thing I could keep my mind on was dodging his attacks. He did not leave much room for us to attack. The few times we were able to swing at him, he was able to move his body quickly enough that we could not hit him.

Heat Jr. and I took a step back. Agrippa took his fighting stance and had his sword hand in the air pointing at us and his other hand on his hip taunting us. The crowd laughed as Agrippa put on a show, Heat Jr. did not like this one bit. He was getting ready to charge in, but I grabbed him by the shoulder.

"Heat, wait. Do you see how relaxed he is? We too must relax. I can see that he is getting to you, but we just have to stay relaxed."

Heat Jr. took a breath in and slowly breathed out. Heat Jr. listened to me, and things seemed to be working out good for us. We were both calm and not breathing heavy, our movements were more precise and under control.

We were keeping up with Agrippa's pace until suddenly, I was too relaxed. I was too calm. I could feel myself going into a trance. The hair on the back of my neck started to stand up. My muscles began to tighten. The movements that were once hard to see, were clear as day now. I went on the offensive. I was able to land five fatal hits on Agrippa before he could even take a step. One on his neck and four holes were placed in his padded armor. The crowd was speechless. Agrippa's eyes widened to twice their normal size.

"I've seen this before; we must get far away!" He threw his coins at us, grabbed his son by the arm, and bolted away from the fighting pits. A few people in the crowd started running, too. The others laughed, because they did not know what they were running from. Heat Jr. took off after Agrippa and was somehow able to catch him. Agrippa spoke to Heat Jr. for a moment. I was unable to hear what was said. After that, Agrippa and his son continued to run. Heat Jr. turned and looked at me and slowly walked back towards me.

"Agrippa says he has seen your trance before on another one of your Foxfang members. He says that the damage that was done by him was so great, he killed everyone in sight." Heat Jr looked at me, sized me up, and laughed. "There is no way a man or Foxfang could be that strong. And if he was as strong as he says he was, how was Agrippa able to get away and tell the story."

While listening to him laugh, I was wondering, who was the other Foxfang he was talking about?

Agrippa's coins were more than plenty to get us horses. We even had enough left over to fill our bellies once more before we headed to the Grey Mountains. We were finally on our way to Heat Jr.'s home. I was a bit nervous, but I felt that we could take on anything after our victory at Dagger Tip. I kept a positive attitude, but Heat Jr. had only revenge on his mind. My blood boiled for him. After eating, we mounted our horses and began to ride.

"So, what is this trance that has everyone so spooked?" Heat Jr. laughed the talk of a trance off, but now he was asking me of it, so he must have believed some of it.

"A trance is when you look deep inside yourself, finding hidden power. You close your eyes, and you see a white light floating about. Catching the white light causes you to slip into the trance. I myself have witnessed the full power of a trance, but have not been able to fully reach that power yet I can't seem to focus enough to catch the light." I was explaining to Heat Jr. the best way that I knew how.

"So when you witnessed this trance, was everyone onsite killed and mountain brought to the ground?"

"There was no one around to kill, but I was told that when you go into a trance your body keeps wanting to fight, and sometimes the only way to bring a person out of a trance is to cut their head off. Some people can control their trance, and others cannot. It was kind of like stringing together a new bow and firing it for the first time. And my first time firing this particular bow, I happened to put a hole in a wall and bring down part of a mountain."

Heat Jr. seemed to be keeping up with me as I was explaining this to him.

"Well, when we get my castle, I might need you to go into a trance, but don't ye be taking down my castle," Heat Jr. said sarcastically. "I honestly wanted to take you to the fighting pits to see if you had any skills at all. Now I know that you can hold your own."

"You tested me? What if I would have died?" I shouted at Heat Jr. in a tone I have never used before.

"Zek, you and I are on our way to face traitorous bastards and grave robbing bandits. If you could not make your way through the fighting pits, I would have turned around and took you back to your village myself."

Heat Jr. was right, but I chose to ride in silence, for I was still angry with him taking a gamble with my life. After riding a ways, Heat Jr. finally spoke again.

"Did you figure out a name for your mount?"

"Name?" I asked. I had never had a pet or any other type of companion, so coming up with a name was difficult for me to do. "I have not."

"Well, you best be thinking of one. It's bad luck to ride through the desert on a horse with no name."

"Etch. How about that? Do you like the name Etch?" I petted his mane and scratched his neck, and the horse seemed to like the name Etch. It meant swift in ancient Foxfang tongue. I did not know much about horses other than they need food and water, but Etch seemed to be very young and manageable. The front part of his body was white, and his hind side was brown with white spots. He was very muscular and seemed to be well taken care of. Now he is mine to look after and care for.

"What did you name your horse?" I asked Heat Jr.

"Scorchis," he replied.

I thought to myself, *Why would he give his horse his family name?*

Then I had to ask because the answer was not clear to me. "Heat? Why give your horse your family's name?"

Heat Jr. cleared his chest and began to speak as if he was a noble lord.

"This horse's name shall be Scorchis, for he is now property of the House of Scorchis from this day forward."

"Property?" I asked.

"Yes. Property." Heat Jr. slapped his horse's side as he said property. The horse reared up and sent Heat Jr. falling off.

"Maybe you guys should be allies," I laughed at Heat Jr. as he laid on the ground and watched his horse run off. He started to walk and the horse eventually came back.

"Whomever trained these horses trained them well," Heat Jr. said with a smirk on his face. He was ever so much right; these horses seemed to like us and respected us if we treated them right and respected them.

It was starting to get dark, and we decided to set up camp for the night. We had been making great time, and it would be good for the horses to rest since water and food in the desert was scarce. Heat Jr. made a fire, and we sat around it as the flames danced in the night. Heat Jr. sat in silence sharpening his sword. As I watched him do this, I could see that he was in deep concentration. If I was going through the same thing he was, I too would have a lot on my mind.

"When my father gave me this sword, I was barely able to walk. He put this sword in my hands and made me take it everywhere. It was forged on the Island of Hammer and Flame. Many works of art came from that island, but this sword was nothing like they have ever seen. My father put the soul of a phoenix in this sword."

As I listened to Heat Jr. tell me about his weapon, I noticed that he was looking in his eyes in the reflection of his sword. He was out for blood and ready to get revenge.

"The first time I killed with this sword, I was only 13. An epic battle came to the doorstep of our castle. I must have killed 40 men that day. I still remember the smell of their flesh burning every time my sword sliced their skin."

Heat Jr. did not notice that he was manipulating the flames of our campfire. He was rambling on and on not paying attention. The flames of the fire started growing larger and larger. They were taller than we sat; the next thing I knew, a small flaming phoenix emerged from the flames. The Phoenix hovered above our heads for a moment and flew high up into the sky until I could not see it anymore. Heat Jr. did not even bat an eye. He startled the horses a little bit, but they did not run off.

I stayed silent for a while. Heat Jr. was thinking of his strategic plan. He was talking to himself under his breath and repeating people's names, ways to get in, and places inside the castle. Heat Jr. drew a map in the dirt to try and better help explain.

"There is an old well behind the castle. We used to play around it when we were children. It may not even be there anymore. This well goes down and leads into the dungeon. We will have to take as many as we can quietly, so we do not raise any eyebrows until we can get into the holding cells to release all of the prisoners they took captive. The few who were still loyal to my father. When we reach them, they can tell us their numbers and what we are up against."

Heat Jr.'s plan sounded simple, but he and I both knew there would be a lot more than just sneaking around we had to do. We just did not know how much sneaking and how many people we were dealing with, which made things a bit more complicated. I believed that we could handle anything that came our way.

We laid down and tried to get some rest; we still had another day of travel before we would be in the mountains. As soon as Heat Jr.'s head hit the ground, he was sound asleep. I stayed up a while longer and watched the flames of our fire die down. As I began to drift off, I started to hear a strange noise. It sounded like people were talking, but in a language I had never heard or could understand. I nudged Heat Jr., but he did not respond. I nudged him again and whispered his name.

He woke up and pulled the Crown of Nightmares halfway off his face. I put my finger over my lips to motion him to be silent and pointed into the direction of the voices. Heat Jr. fixed his ears in the direction then his eyes opened wide.

"We must leave at once!"

By the look on his face as he gathered his things, I knew whatever it was, we had to make haste. We quietly made our way to the horses and the sound of swords being unsheathed was the next thing we heard. There were six hooded figures dressed in black standing next to us with swords drawn. As they stood in front of us not knowing who or what they were, I did know one thing. I knew that we were in the presence of an unnatural evil. Their rags were tattered, and their swords were chipped and battered. I do not think they cared how pretty they looked. They only cared about seeing our blood on the sand.

One of them spoke the words, "Laas das meas douva feina."

I did not understand the meaning, or the tongue it was spoke in.. As they moved towards us, we drew our swords. When Heat pulled his blade, he summoned flames that lit up the night. Heat Jr. used a slash and dodge routine to keep them at bay. Three of them came towards me, bringing their swords back to start their attack. As they brought them forward, I spun around blocking them all and disorientating them. Spinning around was an attempt to kick sand in their faces. I stepped forward and kicked one in the chest and sent it to the ground. I kicked another one of them, but it did not send him to the ground, just slowed him down. As I did that, the one still standing grabbed me by the throat and lifted my feet off the ground. I was face-to-face with a hooded creature that had no face, just a body of rotted bones. I could feel him trying to squeeze the life out of me as his grip got tighter. He snorted in my face and let out a breath of air. His breath smelled of death and rotting flesh. Heat Jr. erupted himself into a ball of flames, setting some of their robes on fire. As they were putting out the flames, we managed to catch up to the startled horses. We

mounted them and rode until the horses could not give any more.

"What the fuck was that!?" I shouted to Heat Jr. Being nearly out of breath, I was not sure if he understood me.

Heat Jr. was sitting on the ground next to his horse, same as me: out of breath.

Heat Jr., finally able to get the words out, said, "Those were Deathbringers. Tormented souls, Faceless Death, Whispers of Evil and servants of The Dark Lord, Obrix."

I read a book on Obrix once. It was full of tales about his corruption and manipulation. It told how he would go and burn villages to the ground, provoking the folks to war against his army that did not fear death. Obrix was a cold-hearted warlord who tried to rule everything his eyes could see. What made things worse, Obrix made games out of his evil encounters. In all my years, Foxfang did all we could to avoid him. I found myself crossing swords with his servants.

"What could they have wanted?" I asked.

"I'm guessing they were on their way to collect souls and ended up crossing swords with us and we ended up on their path of destruction. Fortunate for us, not a hair on our heads were harmed..."

Heat Jr was right. We came face-to-face with Messengers of Darkness, and no harm was done to us. Creatures whose voices were so soft, but only evil words left their tongues. Sleeping anywhere near this area would not be wise. We would have to keep moving until daylight to guarantee our safety from the Deathbringers.

In the distance, the sun was starting to rise over the Grey Mountains. Heat Jr. and I were beat; we did not get a wink of sleep. We had to keep our eyes open for the Deathbringers. We did not see any, but we could not have taken the chance to drop our guard or turn our backs to them for one moment. Heat Jr. steadied the horses while I went to find us a nice place to rest out of travelers' sight and away from the road. I managed to find us a little cave whose opening faced away from the road. It was a perfect place for us to rest for a while. I whistled at Heat Jr. for him to come to me. He used what little energy he had left to bring him and the two horses to me. When Heat Jr. got to where I was, he began to make a fire.

"The sun is about to be up any moment, why would you build a fire right now?" I asked Heat Jr.

"Just in case someone comes, and we don't wake up in time. These flames will protect us."

Heat Jr. was right; he was a master of the flames. If something came close enough to the flames without us waking up, they would meet the Phoenix. We could rest easy for a while. We put one of the horses at the back of the cave to put our heads on. The other horse we put in front of the cave's opening, just in case. We both unsheathed our swords and laid them next to us as we drifted off into the Lillies.

I woke before Heat Jr. When I woke it, was about midday. There was no sun in the sky at this time. Heat Jr.'s fire was still lit and roaring. The sound of downpour hitting rocks and puddles was all there was to be heard. Then the fire went out. While laying there, we were somehow able to get much needed rest. I found it humorous that I was sharing a piece of dirt with the Prince of Flames in a cave. This was no place for the likes of royalty.

While Heat Jr. was tossing and turning, I was thinking about our encounter with the Deathbringers. I relived that moment over and over in my head and tried to think of what I could have done differently. Honestly, there was nothing I could have done differently. We were lucky to make it away from them unscathed. There still felt like there was something more we could have done.

Heat Jr. finally woke up.

"Have you been awake for a while?"

I nodded my head. Heat Jr. stretched and then gathered his things. He was already to be off and on his way. I stopped him.

"Heat... I know we almost there. I am not backing down. I just want to know if you thought about what we are about to do...? We are going to go to war with your kinsmen ..."

Heat Jr. stopped me; he knew where I was going with this conversation. I was going to ask him how could he take the lives of people he loves and grew up with. He stopped me before the words could leave my tongue.

"Zek, I know you don't understand what I'm going through. I have not always been the nicest person, but I have never disobeyed my King's orders. Men that I would call brother took the life of our King. A man who took care of his people. A man we pledged our lives and loyalty to. He was my father."

Heat Jr. was right; I did not understand. If someone were to hurt Shadow or anyone I cared for, there was no telling what I would do. I would probably climb the Ivory Towers and bring war to the King himself. I had no right to judge Heat Jr., nor did I. Heat Jr. had every right to be angry with the people killed his father. I did not have the right answer, but I did support Heat Jr. whatever he decided to do.

The downpour had ended. Out came the sun and dried up all the rain. The dessert went from dry, to wet, and now to this unbearable muggy heat wave. We were both silent. I was not sure why Heat Jr. was not talking. I was waiting for him to speak; I felt I overstepped some boundaries.

"There is something that you don't hear every day." I listened a little harder and could hear the sound of something moving across the sands in the distance. Heat Jr. pointed over to where the sound was

coming from, and I could see a group of people. More people than I could count on two hands. With them, they had creatures that my eyes never had a chance to meet. They were white, horse-like creatures with humps on their backs. The hair where the mane, tail, and around the hoofs had bright flames. Almost the same way as the flames on Heat Jr.'s head. These flames did not seem to bother the men riding them. These creatures seemed to be very calm and moving at a very fast pace. There were two larger of these creatures and two smaller ones. The larger ones had saddles on their backs that resembled carriages and each held about four men inside of them. Long red banner was hung from these carriages bearing a large white eye. If I had to guess, was their tribal crest. The smaller two of these creatures only had one person on them, which seemed to be the leaders.

"Is that a Brother of the Flame I see?" Heat Jr. let out a shout, excited to see his brother from a far. The caravan of travelers turned around and paused. One of the two men ventured closer towards us to get a better look at Heat Jr., who had his arms open on top of his horse.

The man came a little closer and shouted. "Haaahoo!"

Kicking up sand behind them, the two of them raced their mounts across the sands to meet one another.

The other men and I slowly made our way to the reunion of the two. By the time we made it to their celebration, the two of them were off their mounts and greeting. The greeting then turned to laughter, headlocks, and rolling in the sand. When Heat Jr. picked himself up off the ground, he introduced me.

"Zek of the Foxfang Tribe, this is Tranquil Blaze." I found myself shaking hands with a tall dark skin man with blue eyes. He wore his hair like mine. His hand was very warm, like the flames were trying to get out. He looked very solid and wore similar armor to Heat Jr.

"…And this is Unseen Saber." Unseen Saber was a teenage boy who was in serious need of a bathing. His hand was rough and felt like sand. His grip was not as firm as the other man. He was wearing what seemed to be wyrm scales. Extremely valuable, but he had them covered in filth.

These two strangers looked very harmless, but there was something more to them that I was not going to ask Heat Jr. just yet. The scent of Blaze's magic was similar to Heat Jr.'s, but not as strong. Saber's magic was like nothing I have smelled before. Instead of smelling him next to me I could smell him all around me.

"Foxfang? You are a long way from home, my friend." Tranquil Blaze spoke in a deep voice.

"Mr. Tranquil, I'm surprised you have heard of it. Not many have."

"Please Zek, no need to be proper with your words. We are here in the desert. No one speaks proper in the desert. It is not as if someone will lash out at you for not being proper." He sarcastically spoke in a nobleman's voice. "Call me Blaze."

The burden of upsetting my new friends was lifted off my shoulders. Now I was faced with showing them that I was not a stuck-up simpleton who was full of myself. I heard them laughing and whispering among themselves. I knew from this point forward, they would not be able to let me talking proper down.

"Have we been to the Foxfang Village?" Saber asked

"No, we have not. Just really close, and we've heard many interesting stories." Blaze replied. I wondered what interesting stories he may have heard. Then, thinking more on the matter, he would not find his everyday life interesting, but I would probably find it fascinating. "So, are you heading home, my ol' friend?" Blazed asked Heat Jr., but Heat Jr. did not reply. "Ah. I see. Family politics," Blaze said.

Saber sighed.

"I would hardly call that politics. Dictatorship by hostile takeover? That's political as it gets. Heat, I'm hurt you will not let me show them the inside of a sandstorm." Saber had worked himself up. It would seem that he thought little of the things to come out of his mouth.

Blaze put his hand on Saber's shoulder. It was an attempt to calm him down, but he was already too far gone.

Heat Jr. let out a deep breath.

"It truly is not your fight. I picked the right army to go with me. Besides, enough people have been hurt." Heat Jr. was trying to be calm and not set Saber off more. Everything Heat Jr. said was not what Saber wanted to hear.

"So, this Foxfang. Is he your army?" Saber asked, spit flying out his mouth. For a young man, he had a pretty bad temper.

It was clear the three of them had known each other for quite some time. I myself wondered why Heat Jr. chose me to travel with. Hearing Saber speak drew my attention to a more important question. If people were offering us help, why would he not take their help? Heat Jr. either was full of pride, wanted no help from anyone, and was going to get us slaughtered. Or he had a miracle tucked somewhere he was not telling anyone.

Saber went on and on about lending us their swords. He tore up his face in many expressions. His voice was getting louder and louder. Blaze was trying to calm him. Heat Jr. was trying to persuade him. I was moments away from putting my fist right where the noise was coming from.

…And then all of a sudden, he stopped. Saber was silent but had a look on his face like he was innocent. Moments ago, he was raising sin, and now nothing.

"He did it again," Heat Jr. said.

Blaze's dark face lit up. All his teeth were showing, his smile was so big.

"Saber's memory isn't right. He has short-term and long-term memory loss. He gets himself so worked up and angry that he forgets things. Now he's embarrassed he showed his ass and can't remember."

I was confused. Never had I met a person with both short-term and long-term memory lost. Seeing Saber stand about cluelessly started to make sense.

"Have we been to the Foxfang village?" Saber asked. The looks on everyone's face was speechless. Saber was confused; we had already talked about this moments ago. Blaze and Heat Jr. rode off in laughter, leading the caravan. No amount of gold could not measure anything close to seeing the smile on the Prince of Flame's face in such a pressing time in his life.

While traveling with Saber and Blaze, I learned much about them. They were nomads, Keepers of the Sands. They were following Sand Wyrms through the desert before we met. It was the time of year after mating season for the Sand Wyrms. The female Sand Wryms travel in a clew, or clat, days ahead of the males. The males, being tired from mating rituals and mating, travel a much slower pace behind the females. The Keepers of the Sands only killed one male ,and not the Alpha. Killing the Alpha would make the other males fight amongst themselves more than they already had to during mating season.

The Keepers of the Sands had been around for quite some time from my understanding. I had never read anything about them or heard Shadow mention them. Then again, I was from the forest, and the forest was the only thing I knew much about. Blaze told me of their master hunting skills and many rare and large game that they had killed. He also told me of their many battles with bandits and how they kept the sands safe.

The more Blaze talked, the more I realized how much the Keepers of the Sands and the Foxfang had in common. Like us, they respected their elders and put them first. Their elder was the Queen of Trade. She lived somewhere next to Barter's Bay, where the desert met the seas. They were very peaceful people, who had the means to protect themselves if violence came their way, as were us Foxfang.

"Don't make a sound!" Saber snapped at everyone. Saber hopped off his mount and put his ear to the ground. The other men ready their nets and weapons.

"Sorry. Thought I heard a Sand Wyrm."

As we rode across the sands of the desert my ears became more and more full of knowledge about the Keepers of the Sands. Blaze and Saber talked my ear off. I finally asked what they called the creatures they rode. They called them Flameles Candles of the Sands. Through conversation after conversation, I knew all their relatives four generations back. I knew migration patterns. I knew what to eat in the desert and what not to eat. I knew the Keepers of the Sands' meeting spots in case they were to split up. I even knew what foods made Saber's stomach turn. They talked, laughed, and cried until the sun went down.

We kept onward until we could find a nice sandy hill to put our backs to. The others set up camp, and Blaze explained to me strategically why they set their backs to the sands. With your back against the sand you can feel Sand Wyrms tunneling if they are near. There would also be one lookout at the top of the hill dressed in Scales of the Sand Wyrm. We were to each take a turn keeping an eye out for any activity, while the others tried to rest their eyes. My eyes had seen Deathbringers. I doubted they would be able to rest.

A warm hand grabbed my shoulder. "Zek, wake up. It's your turn to keep watch." Heat Jr. spoke to me in a voice loud enough only I could hear. I woke and saw the others around me sleeping. I guess my eyes were able to rest. Heat handed me the Scales of the Sand Wyrm so I could blend in with the sands. "Keep your eyes open, my friend. I know you know what is out there."

I nodded my head. If he was speaking of the Deathbringers, then I knew. I made my way to the top of the hill to sit, watch, and wait for anything to move besides the desert sand.

The night was calm. The stars in the sky lit the way to the mountains to which we are heading. They seemed to be sitting low, almost appearing to touch their jagged edges and sharp peaks.

"The Grey Mountains…" I whispered to myself. That was our destination. That will be the place where we make things right, in the name of Heat. The Grey Mountains could be our resting place, if we were not careful.

I sat and watched the night. The faint sound of people tossing and turning was behind me, and the sounds of creatures from the night were around me. I was not frightened by the sounds. I did not really pay attention to them. I was more focused on the smell of death. For I knew if we saw them again, they would not be so quick to give up.

Looking at the Grey Mountains reminded me of my time with the Night Fox. I kept thinking of the raw power he had showed me. If I could show a display of that energy now, we would not have to travel and fight. I would be able to turn that mountain to sand. But that was a hallucination I had, and things like that did not happen in my life.

Besides, I am certain Heat Jr. planned on killing them one by one. Killing them from a distance would be too easy. I am very sure he wants to see the life leave their eyes, for wronging his father. Then again, I could have been very wrong.

I could be very wrong indeed. What if Heat decided to take the Torturer's Approach? I once read a book called *The Torturer's Approach*. This was a book about a farmer who worked for a noble town. This farmer worked harder than any shopkeeper, blacksmith, or merchant, and still did not have enough or make enough for his family's needs. He worked this way season after season. Year after year. With no muss, no fuss, until one day, he went to ask the king for help. He was denied, and this angered the farmer. He set into motion what he thought was a brilliant plan. He dusted the towns people's crops with poison that would paralyze them, so that only him and his family would be safe.

Everyone went on living their busy lives. Few days went by; the children started to become ill. Soon after, everyone else followed. The whole town was paralyzed. The farmer wasted no time and went straight to work. He started with the king. He sat the king down and then started to chop, hack, bleed, and slice his family right in front of him.

The book went on about how the farmer went from harvesting crops to harvesting souls. He tortured the whole town in 20 days. None of the deaths were the same. There was probably 600 in the town. What if Heat was our farmer?

I could feel my face forcing a smile. As much as I wanted to believe that Heat Jr. would not torture them, the thought was still there in my head. *When it comes to people hurting your loved ones, there is no telling how one would act.* My blood boiled for Heat Jr., and in that same moment, chills ran up and down my spine. I had never killed anyone. In defense, yes, but I had not maliciously assaulted anyone. I hoped Heat Jr.'s reason for me being here was not to torture. My mind went blank.

Footsteps were coming up the hill behind me. Listening to the steps closer, I realized it was Heat Jr. He walked on the tips of his toes more than anyone I had ever known. I guess when you were able to move fast as the flames, you would always be on your toes and quick to act.

"You realize you were up here all night and no one else got a chance at watch duty?"

I looked behind me to see Heat Jr. Behind him, I could see the top of the sun coming up over the forest in the distance. After this hill I will be lost in this sea of sand.

"The men are not complaining about a good night's rest."

"But I'm worried about you." Heat's voice began to get louder. "When you are traveling with a companion, you stick to the plan. What part of our plan had you star gazing and Maker knows what else?"

A few eyes made their way to the top of the hill where we were having a conversation. Heat Jr. grabbed the back of my neck to pull my ear closer.

"I don't trust any of their followers down there, Zek. I was gonna tell you about the bad feeling I was getting from them on our next shift rotation, but you never made it back down. If you are not a Brother of the Flame, I do not trust you." Heat Jr. paused. "Zek, all I'm saying is, I only trust my brothers. You, brother, are the only one I know I can rely on."

I did not reply with words. My eyes focused on Blaze and Saber's followers, to see if I could sense it, too. I sniffed the air to see if I could smell any magic. There was none, but I kept my guard up. I patted Heat Jr. on the back as a gesture of understanding.

Heat Jr. began to lead me down the hill. Before we made it with in ears reach, I asked, "Do you really think we have to be worried about these men? They rode by our sides, laughed, and joked for many of stretch of sand with us. Do you really think they would do us harm?"

"My friend," Heat Jr. said with a smile. "You have been in the forest for too long."

"All my life," I replied.

Heat Jr. smile grew bigger.

"And that, my friend, is why I like you. You are innocent. But outside the forest, people forget about the things that matter and teachings. They focus more on themselves and gold. Please believe me, and remember when I say people will do the dirtiest things to you just to line their pockets with gold. You are the opposite, and I respect that."

By the time we got to the bottom of the hill everyone was up and readying their mounts. Saber was standing the closest to the hill, I am guessing him standing the closest meant he was concerned the most.

"Is everything alright? You two kiss and make up?" His face showed concern and worry, but his tone was sarcastic. The few ears that heard began in laughter.

Heat Jr. lightly jabbed under Saber's chin.

"Yes, just a lover's quarrel," Heat Jr. joked.

I cracked half a smile to try and fit in with the other laughing faces around me. I was not sure how Heat Jr. could accuse these men of wronging us and then batting an eye and joking around with them. He was right; I had been in the forest for much too long. I did not understand the ways of these men.

I was the last to mount. I watched everyone before I mounted. Shadow's words echoed in my head. *Always be aware of your surroundings.* I patted Etch's neck.

"Are you ready, my friend?" Etch shook his head motioning he was not ready. I gave his reins a tug. He did not budge. "What's wrong, my friend?" I asked while stroking his mane. Etch snorted and stomped his hoof on the ground. "Are you hungry?" Etch motioned that he was not hungry. "Are you thirsty?" Etch motioned no, that he was not thirsty. "Is there something wrong?"

Etch snorted and shook his head yes. My eyes widened, growing a whole size bigger. Etch sensed Heat Jr.'s bad feeling also. I just could not tell which one of these followers was wronging us.

"We're moving out, Foxfang!" Blaze shouted out from the front of the caravan. I hopped on Etch, but he would not move. "Come on, my friend, let us ride." As I spoke those words, Etch began to move, but at the pace of a stump beetle. We were already a few strides behind the caravan. My patience was starting to wear thin with Etch. A few heads turned to look at Etch's display. The turned heads began to smile, and then the desert was full of laughter.

This continued for a few more strides. Etch moved slowly until we were just right behind the caravan, not in it. Then he started to pick up his pace into normal strides.

"What is with you?" I asked.

Etch did not make any sounds; he just kept his pace and his distance from the caravan. I could hear the followers in the caravan laughing and shouting out obscenities about my horse. Heat Jr. glanced over his shoulder, and I could see him smirk. Was everyone really getting that much of titter from watching my horse disobey me?

"Alright, I have had enough!" Heat Jr. shouted, and the laughter stopped. "Have you never seen a man on a new horse?" Heat Jr. snapped.

"A man, aye, but never a dog," one of the followers cracked. Heat Jr. started to laugh under his breath and then hopped off his horse. He walked over to the speaker of those words and stopped right in front of his flamel. He stood in silence looking the man in the eyes. Moments later Heat Jr. pulled the man's sword from his flamel's side pouch.

Jaws dropped and a few of the followers moved in closer, with hands on their swords. Saber seemed shocked. He was two shades lighter, like he saw a ghost, or was about to see the making of a few ghosts. A frown found his face when he looked over at Blaze. Blaze did nothing or said nothing. Blaze sat on his mount with his arms folded and half a smile on his face.

Heat Jr. whispered to the follower with flames in his eyes.

"You would not last two rounds with this 'dog.' I bet; you could not even go a full round with your mother's cunt."

Heat Jr. swung the sword around and pretended to be a skilled knight. A few of the followers got a rise from this anecdote. Blaze more than the anyone else did, laughing at Heat Jr. taunting one of his followers. He was chuckling so hard that he was losing his breath.

Heat Jr. continued to mock and taunt the man, hoping he would step down from his horse. The once moments ago loudmouth was now silent. The laugh had run away from his face. He was now wearing no facial expression, and his cheeks were redder than the leaves on a Risclub Tree.

By the time Etch and I joined the gathering of foolishness, Blaze had tears streamed from his eyes. The poor man was still on his flamel getting teased by Heat Jr.. The man was moments away from having tears stream down his face, until Blaze saved him.

"Enough!" Blaze shouted over the laughs, and the caravan was silent. Heat Jr. continued to jibe briefly. When he became bored, he threw the sword to the ground and kicked sand on it. When he hopped off his flamel to pick it up, Heat Jr. lunged at him, making him flinch. He was so spooked, he fell backwards in the sand.

Blaze slapped his thigh and laughed.

"That's what happens when you go pissing off royalty," he roared over everyone in the caravan laughing. His dark skin began to glow red.. It would seem he was overheating from laughing. Heat Jr. walked back to his horse. All the followers said nothing, but their eyes were saying 'I do not want to be next' to Heat Jr. When Heat Jr. hopped on his horse, there was a loud commotion. The followers that surrounded him were all running around in a frenzy. I hopped off my horse to help Heat Jr., but before I got close enough, it was too late.

"Anger Asp!" Blazed cried at the top of his lungs. I read about the Asp of Rage, but never saw one. Depending on your whereabouts, they are many things; it could also be called Anger Asp or Red Belly Slitherer. They do not look like much, but they are small and can be vicious. They are black and have red spirals on their back. Their head has one large, red diamond. The eyes are bright orange, and their bellies are deep red. It is said then when the asp bites a victim, they do not get sick from the poison; they just become truly angry.

Someone had put the asp in Scorchis's side pouch. When Heat Jr. hopped on to his horse, he must have angered the asp before he was bitten in the side of his leg. Heat Jr. let out a battle cry and pulled out his sword. Heat Jr.'s sword burst into flames, glowing red hot. Heat threw it at the man in front of him. The sword was so hot, it went through the man's chest, searing everything in its path. The sword was so powerful it did not stop…

The man behind the seared victim was not safe either. The sword continued on a path of destruction, cutting his arm off. I, being next in its path, was lucky enough to dodge it. I managed to save my head; I could hear flames as the blade went past my face. Heat Jr. let out another battle cry and his sword came to a halt. Moments after that, the sword starts whipping back towards Heat Jr. Everyone scattered around like flies, hoping not to be the next victim of what would seem like an unstoppable blade.

The sword made it back to its master. Heat Jr. being this angry made the ground around him warm. Blaze and all his followers drew their weapons. Four of the men went in to try and detain Heat Jr., but they all fell short. One by one he barbarically beat their faces. I ran over to where Blaze.

"I've seen these snake bites, but never on someone who possesses so much power." Blaze pointed at Heat Jr. as he brought his followers to submission.

"We're going to have to show him the inside of a storm, or he will

kill us all," Saber snapped.

"No! The inside of a storm will kill him." Blaze tore his face up, for he did not want to harm his friend, but at the same time, his friend was slaughtering his friends and followers..

"Well, you handle it your way, and if that doesn't work, then I will show him," Saber nodded and then waited for Blaze to reply. There was a long pause between the two that felt like 100 years. Blaze finally gave Saber a nod. You could tell Blaze did not agree, but Saber's option was Blaze's only option.

Blaze let out a sigh. A fight with Heat Jr. was not what he wanted.

"Zek, you must go and search for Bean Nuts. Grind them down, and somehow get him to breathe in some of their dust. Low growing bush with dark brown leaves. They usually grow on the shaded side of rocks. Only grab the ones with tender shells. Make haste!"

Doing as I was told, I hopped on Etch and rode as fast the winds could take me. Behind me, I could hear the clashing of swords, and the screams of men who were fighting for their lives. People tell stories about monsters to scare children. I was witness to one of the scariest monsters I had ever seen. No story could prepare me for this. Heat Jr.'s sword was too much for them to handle. Flawless blade skills in one hand and the hottest flames known to man in the other. Blaze and his followers had their hands full; each time one approached Heat Jr., he did not hesitate to bring them to the ground.

While riding, I started to notice there were hardly any rocks to be seen in the desert. I was sent to go find a needle in a haystack, but realistically, it was more like finding a pebble in a sea. I rode for what felt like a lifetime before finding my first rock. I came up short and there was nothing to be found. I searched high and low. Everywhere I looked, looked like the places I looked last time or the time before that. There were rocks, but only a few big enough to cast a shadow. The ones that did cast a shadow did not have the items I sought. My nerves were on the edge. My friends' lives were depending on how fast I could find something I have only heard of but never laid eyes on. I am sure anyone in my position would be losing their breeches right now. Pit, I am sure any tavern ruffian would have lost his ale. After he seen a flaming sword make its way through the person's body you were just sharing laughs with. A "horror story" is the only real way to describe what I saw. I could describe the events in great details, and no one would believe a word.

Who cares if anyone believed me! I had to save Blaze and his followers from Heat Jr.'s wrath. After I did that, Blaze would tell people. He was an honest man; people would believe him.

A ROCK! I saw it sitting on top of a hill to the left of me. I turned Etch in the direction of the hill and bolted, not wasting a moment of time. When we got there, after the first few steps up the hill, the sands began to collapse beneath us. I hopped off Etch and made the rest of the way to the top on foot. When I made it to the top of the hill to check the shaded side of the rock, I saw the Bean Nuts lying on the ground. Someone had already been here. They cut the limbs of the off the small bush and left the nuts laying in a small pile on the ground. I found this to be very strange. I looked around the area for any clues. Some type of sign of the person who did this or which direction they went. There were none.

Being on top of this hill, I was able to get a better look at the desert around me. In the direction I came from, I could still see the flames still flying from Heat Jr.'s fury off in the distance. How I wish I could help, but gathering Bean Nuts was my way of assisting. It was not even midday yet, and the sun was beaming down like it was working twice as hard before supper. The air felt heavy, like it was weighing down your lungs with each breath you took in. When the wind blew, it did not really give off a breeze. When the wind blew, it was more like dragon breath on the skin. Even though the desert was a harsh environment, I somehow enjoyed it. I did not enjoy that everything I saw or touched could kill my vibe, but the scenery was nice.

To the right of me was another rock on top of a hill. I motioned to Etch to meet me at the bottom of the hill. He made it to the bottom before I could, so halfway down the hill, I jumped on to his back. As soon as I stuck my landing, we were off. We made our way across the sands with great speed. As soon as we reached the bottom of the hill, I hopped off. I did not even bother running up because the sand would slow me down. I took three leaps and landed myself at the top. A FUCKING MIRAGE!

I sat on the ground and pouted like a child who did not finish their supper. We all know if you do not finish your supper; you get no dessert. I felt like someone took my dessert and gave it to a fat cousin. I know there were more important things that my mind should be focusing on right now, but I did not care. I was angry. I let my eyes play tricks on me and came up short. I picked my self-pitying ass off the ground. The combination of lack of water and my brain cooking inside my skull was leading to me seeing things. I did not need to sit. I needed to be in motion, searching for Bean Nuts. I hopped back on Etch and continued my search.

After the self-inflicting blood boiling was over, I had a clear head and was able to focus. The mirage had me so riled up, I stopped focusing on saving my friends' lives. It is funny how the sun will affect you. If I did not find the Bean Nuts soon, I might be in for more mirages. That would not be good. The only thing that bothered me now was, I wondered, were my friends alright? I was so far away now that I could not see the flame of the sword anymore. The sooner I got back, the better it would be for everyone.

I found myself paused for a moment. Looking around, I felt like I been to this place before, but I was quite sure I have not. I checked to see if there was someone else's footsteps around…

There was not…

I checked behind me to see if I had walked over my footsteps…

I did not.

Something strange was going on. Next, I knew Etch yanked his head and started heading for another hill. He moved so fast, it felt like he pulled my arm off. Etch maneuvered his way up the hill and to the top without me taking a tumble. When we reached the top of the hill, there on the ground lied a Bean Nut bush pulled from its soil. I quickly hopped off Etch and brought my nose to the bush. I did not touch the bush, so that I could just smell the violator who did this. They left no scent. My nose was full of the sweet, earthy smell of Bean Nuts. I looked around. Down the back side of the hill were footprints. I brought my nose to the footprint to see if I could smell anything. Usually in the woods, people walked around barefooted, so when they left footprints, you would sometimes get a whiff of their sweaty foot. Sometimes the sweaty foot picks up dirt or scents from other places. This footprint had none of that. This person was wearing boots, and they left no smell.

"Who are they?" I whispered under my breath.

I put the Bean Nuts in my side sack and started my way back. As I made my way back to Heat Jr., I thought about the Bean Nuts pulled from the ground. The words *Who are they?* echoed in my head. I thought about how Shadow would have handled the situation. Had it been him, he probably would not have rushed back to Heat Jr.'s aid until he figured out why the roots were pulled. Laughing at his old stubbornness, I felt I was doing the right thing. Heat Jr. was literally ripping us to pieces. I feared if I did not get back soon, I was going to have to take Heat Jr. alone by myself. The thought of that frightened me.

We rode on as if Obrix's hounds were on our heels. I could feel Etch's body starting to fatigue. He probably started tiring ages ago. When he started to slow down, I would whisper, "I'm counting on you, friend, our friends are counting on us." Those words seemed enough to keep him going.

I knew little to none about horses and how much they could endure. In my village, we did not have the need for horses. Most trails were either too narrow or required some type of tree climbing. I honestly had not kept track with the distance Etch and I traveled; so many other things were going through my mind at the time. Now that we saw Heat Jr.'s flames in the distance, all the things in my mind were soon about to be in front of my face.

There was only Saber, Blaze, and one other man from their caravan left. Heat Jr. had been working us over really well. When we got within ear's reach of Blaze, he shouted,

"Grind 'em into a powder and make him breathe them in!"

My insides were tickled a little bit. *Oh yes, just walk up to the Prince of Flames while he hacks and slashes madly. Then have him breathe in the Bean Nuts?* One of those things easier said than done. Shadow always had a saying; *Sarcasm killed the cat.* Not sure what it meant, and I am pretty sure not even Shadow knew what it meant. All I know is that every time someone caught themselves being wise with him, he would say that and put them into their place. I am sure Heat Jr. had more than enough to put me in my place after even thinking a comment like that.

I grabbed the Bean Nuts from my side pouch and hopped off. I held the nuts in my hand so tight that their tender little shells were cracking and were one step closer to being into powder. I ran towards Heat Jr. The person that stood before me resembled nothing of my Brother of the Flame. Flames were pouring out of his eyes. The flames on his head were standing up and gave off a bright orangish-white glow. He was giving off too much heat; it was going to be extremely hard to get in close and have him breathe anything in.

Heat Jr. approached me, sword in his right hand, fist balled tight in the other. His breathing was so deep and heavy, like a growl. The flaming ball of Heat was coming towards me. He kept getting hotter and hotter as he walked towards me. I stood my ground, getting ready for whatever happened next. The heat wave stopped, and Heat Jr. leapt right at me, so fast he was like a beast on its prey. I managed to move out the way without dropping the Bean Nuts.

"I'm not going to lift my sword to you!" I shouted.

"We already lifted our swords and look how many died! You gonna dance around more and get hacked limb from limb, or let me show him the Eye of a Storm?" Saber did not want to kill Heat Jr., but Heat Jr. was leaving us no other option. I nodded to Saber. Saber threw his sword into the ground and motioned us to get back. Blaze put his sword away, you could tell he did not want to use it.

Saber lifted his arms. His skin turned rough and golden like the sand. The sandy figure stood in front of us and dropped to the ground. Saber's clothes laid next to a pile of what seemed to be Saber. A light gust of wind pushed the pile of sand. The pile of sand blew into two lines around Heat Jr. When the two lines connected on the other side of Heat Jr., they formed an eye.

The wind started to blow violently, and the pile of sand that was Saber and the sand from the surrounding area was in the air and ripping around like tiny daggers. Saber had shown Heat Jr. the inside of a sandstorm.

I could not believe my eyes. Saber actually had the ability to make a sandstorm. Everything outside the eye was unaffected. Everything inside the of the eye was.violently tossed around and ripped to shreds.

Everything but Heat Jr. Heat Jr. still had enough strength in him to keep walking inside of the sandstorm. Heat Jr. was trying to walk his way out of the eye.

"What are you waiting for? Toss those Bean Nuts into the storm."

To answer his question, I do not know why I was waiting for, probably the stupidest thing I had ever done. I took my empty hand and flattened the Bean Nuts, moved my hands back forth a few times and tossed them into the storm. Heat Jr. took a few more steps and was almost to the outside of the storm. It would seem the Bean Nuts were not working.

"Ox breath!" Blaze said.

The Bean Nuts must have been grinded too fine. Heat Jr. took another step and lifted his hands to try and rip a hole in the storm. He struggled and struggled until his fingers broke free. He tried harder to make the hole bigger and began to choke.

"It's working!" Blaze shouted.

Heat Jr. continued to choke and fell to his knees. The flames on his head started to die down. Heat Jr. coughed violently, then fell face down into the sand. The sandstorm continued but started to die down. When it was finished, Saber was sitting next to his pile of clothing with his legs folded.

"What do you think, Foxfang?"

"I am impressed," which I really was.

Saber smiled, "I am impressed myself. Usually, the *Eye of the Storm* is a very painful experience ending with a very painful death. Heat Jr. didn't seem to be in pain or die. I am impressed."

"Thank the Maker he didn't rip his way out of the storm," Blaze said while wiping sweat from his forehead.

"Why is that?" I asked.

"Like Saber was saying, that usually ends in a very painful death. Heat showed no sign of weakness and managed to rip his fingers through. Had he got through, could you imagine two flaming heat waves fighting in the desert?"

I shook my head no.

"I honestly don't know what would have happened, but I know it wouldn't have been pretty. But what I do know," Blaze turned his attention to Saber. " I know I never want to see someone that close to leaving a sandstorm again." Blaze said with a smile.

Saber hopped off the ground and began to put his clothes on. He did not find any humor in Blaze's comment.

"He has a few hundred years of experience on me," Saber began to say.

Blaze erupted into laughter.

"And might I add, he is the Prince of Flames. Can't just go around killing princes."

I rushed over to Heat Jr. I rolled his body over. He was out cold. I lifted him up carefully and put him on the back of Scorchis.

Blaze and his remaining man searched for anything of value. There was not much left over from his fallen men. Everything that Heat Jr.'s flames touched was melted to the point that you could hardly even recognize anything.

"Tie the remaining mounts to each other. We are almost to our destination and then we will part ways."

I tied Scorchis to Etch. Saber rounded up all the others, and then we made our way to the well of Heat Jr.'s childhood.

Finally, we arrived!" Saber said and then kissed the ground. Nothing fancy about this place, and from the looks of it, no one had been here for a long time. Just a well and a few trees tucked away in the desert where the hills started to become steeper and sand started to have tiny rocks and pebbles in it. This was one of the signs we were close to the mountains.

"I'm not sure how I found this place. I must have picked up some memories while I was whipping up a storm. I wonder how much I lost?"

I could not tell if Saber was being funny or serious. Either way, I was concerned because I never heard of having short-term-long-term memory loss. Now seeing that Saber could become a sandstorm, it made sense.

Each time he used his Sandstorm, he could possibly lose his memories or gain someone else's from the sand. Not sure if you can call that a loss. He was able to navigate us here, this well, a place from Heat Jr.'s youth, a place Saber never been before, I would call that a gain.

"Get a fire going. We don't want anything sneaking up on our backs." Blaze was right. Even though our numbers were thin. We still had to pull it together and defend ourselves at all cost.

"We will also take turns keeping watch. I'll go first, the rest of you get some rest." Blaze made his way up to the peak of one of the sandy hills.

We did as instructed. Saber circled the camp, checking for food and foes. The other man from the caravan started the fire. I carefully got Heat Jr. off his mount and laid him down with his head slightly raised. I looked at Heat Jr's asp bite, two tiny holes on the outside of his left leg.

"What is your name?" I asked the man making a fire.

A moment of silence set between us.

"Do you know anything about treating an asp wound?"

More silence.

He had a problem, and I was not going to make his problem my problem. I went on about what I was doing

"No. The name is Ordon," he scuffed

One of the asp fangs still appeared to be in his leg. It was in there pretty good. Heat Jr. was sweating, running a fever. The flames on his head were out, but his skin was still burning up. I was not sure if this is normal or not, him being the Prince of Flames. I ripped a piece of Heat Jr. shirt and got it ready to tie around his leg after I plucked the fang.

I began yanking on the tiny fang. Heat Jr. flinched and squirmed, but he still did not come to. I let the fang go. My claws were on it too long and were starting to get hot. I let my paws rest for a bit and then tried again. This time, I spit on his leg, thinking that it would cool his leg down. I was wrong. Ordon began in laughter.

"I asked if you knew how to treat an asp wound. Are you going to help?"

I did not think so. Ordon either had muck for brains, or did not care.

What I did do instead of cooling it down was make steam. This loosened up the fang, and I was able to pull it out with ease. Beads of sweat ran down Heat Jr.'s face. I pinched my claws on the two tiny holes to make sure everything was out of it and then wrapped his leg nice and tight. After a few moments of panting heavily, Heat Jr. was snoring. I decided to save the fang and show it to Heat Jr. when he woke up.

"What's your story?" I asked Ordon.

He looked up from the fire.

"My story is my own," he said.

"What is with you?" I asked firmly.

"The des—" Ordon began.

Saber walked up with an arm full of twigs for the fire and some kind of desert fruit. He tossed Ordon and I each one of the fruits and dropped the sticks next to the fire.

Saber mocked Ordon and finished his sentence, "—the desert is a dangerous place. Members of the caravan expendable. It is best not to get close to outsiders. Save it. Okay we had a few men die by thirst. But how was I supposed to know how thirsty they were if they did not speak?"

Saber whistled at Blaze. He shook his hand and motioned to the fruit as if he were going to toss it. Blaze shook his head no and returned to sentry position.

"We patrol the deserts looking for bandits, hunting wyrms, and fulfilling our Queen's will. Yes, it is dangerous, but this one time, tell him. Our own friend almost killed us moments ago."

"His friend," Ordon said, pointing at me sternly. Then, Ordon sat in silence and gave us a look like he did not really want to. Saber glared at Ordon, and Ordon cleared his throat. "I come from an island far away from here. Me and my people live on Mammoth Mountain. We study the art of Blood Magic. I joined this caravan to give my life... purpose if you will?"

"The desert's dangerous," Saber said.

I swallowed hard. Blood Magic is forbidden. If he gets a taste of your blood, he could cast any spell you have learned. People who study Blood Magic usually drained their victims dry... I wonder why Blaze and Saber would be traveling with the likes of him.

"My mother's n—"

"I think he gets it," Saber said.

"Well, you asked," Ordon said, and folded his arms.

"Son of a bitch!" I shouted. I jumped at Ordon, grabbing his shirt and pinning him to the ground.

Saber was on my heels. His boyish hands grabbed my shoulders, but he was not strong enough to pull me off. Blaze was not far behind him.

"What is the meaning of this?" he whispered loudly, trying not to be too loud in the desert night.

I punched Ordon one good time and sent him into the Lillies.. I literally tried to put my fist through his face. I let go of his shirt and grabbed his arm.

"THIS."

It was the same bite marks that Heat Jr. had. I felt Saber's grip loosen, and then he took a few steps back until he was shoulder to shoulder with Blaze. We all were silent for a moment.

"We have ourselves a predicament," Blaze said.

"What are we going to do with him?" Saber asked.

"We'll wait for the Prince to wake up. He'll decide," Blaze replied, shaking his head.

Saber grabbed rope from his mount. He kicked Ordon in the stomach and then tied his hands and feet together behind his back.

Heat Jr. stayed asleep for four days. While he was asleep, Blaze told all about the people of Scorchis Mountain. Blaze had even been a part of their fold and stayed in the castle. Hence his name and his ability to manipulate flames. He foresaw these traitorous acts long before anyone else, but no one believed him. So, Blaze exiled himself from their kingdom and join the Queen's Caravan He said he did not feel right not taking orders. He was a good judge of character. He said the Trade Queen had a righteous heart. All she really cared about is helping people. Her orders consisted of hunting exotic game and keeping the sands safe for travelers.

He told me they would keep calling Heat Prince, until he called himself The King of Flames. He told stories of Heat Jr.'s father, The King of Flames. They had only good things to say about him, which had me confused to why anyone would want to harm him or even kill him for that matter. I suspected Ordon had something to do with Heat Jr.'s father's death, and now he was coming back to kill the son.

We did not harm Ordon; we just left him tied up in blistering desert sun for four days until Heat Jr. finally woke up.

Although on the second day Blaze and I listened to Saber talk about the many ways he would beat Ordon until his life was just hanging by threads. I had enough after his first five scenarios; I wanted his mouth shut. Although I did find it funny when Saber spoke of tossing Ordon into the well and letting him face whoever is on the other side.

Blaze said The Trade Queen is going to think he is not able to lead after hearing this. I knew he had a lot on his mind. One of Blaze's members of his fold tried to kill one of his Brothers of the Flame and possibly getting his rank stripped. He had a lot on his mind, indeed. Saber talking did not help. So, we sat and listen to Saber talk until Heat Jr. woke.

When Heat Jr. finally woke up, the first thing we did was tell him everything. We told him about the asp. We told him about the accidental slaughter. About confronting the traitor. How we did not question him until the prince wished to speak with him. How we did not seriously hurt him until the prince wanted to hurt him. Heat Jr. found that very funny. He figured we would have laid to waste with him already. We told him everything that led us to where we were now.

We all walked over to where Ordon was. Heat Jr. led the way. The whole time, he sat outside the shade. When the first sun came up, it was on him. When the last of the sun went down, it was on him. His appearance looked like he was dragged behind a horse. His mouth was dry, and his lips were cracked from the little to no water Saber gave him. Skin was burnt, eyes dazed and barely open. When Heat Jr. stopped walking, Saber took a bow and acted if he was some type of noble's servant.

Heat Jr. untied Ordon's feet from his hands, but left his hands behind his back. Heat Jr. stood right above him and waited until Ordon made eye contact before speaking.

"So, you didn't speak for four days. You either have already thought of what you're going to say, or you're not going to say anything at all, correct?"

Ordon's dried out face tried to smile at Heat Jr. He looked down and spit at Heat Jr's boots.

"Been waiting four days to do that," Ordon whispered.

Heat Jr. smiled.

"Just tell me who hired you to kill me and why, and you can go home tonight."

Ordon coughed roughly.

"You weren't the target. The Fox was."

Everyone was silent. You could hear jaws drop. Blaze was the first to act. He jumped forward at Ordon, and before he could get to him, Heat Jr. put his hand up, and Blaze halted. Blaze fixed his mouth as if he were about to speak, but Heat Jr. shook his head no. Heat Jr. folded his arms and stood in silence, disgusted with Ordon.

I did not know what to think. Why would anyone want me dead? What had I done to make someone want to put a contract out on me?

"Who gave you the contract?" Heat Jr. asked.

"I don't know his name. He was just a fox dressed in all black. He gave me half of the gold then and said he would give me the other half

after the Foxfang was bitten."

Heat Jr., Blaze and Saber argued amongst themselves while I said nothing and thought.

I thought about who would want me dead. No one name came to mind. I thought on it more and more. While I thought, they bickered amongst themselves, seeing who would get the first blow. How they were going to end him. Insulting him and his family name to no end. Finally, I had enough thinking, and with the noise they were making, I could not process a proper thought.

I reached out to Heat Jr.'s shoulder.

"May I?" I asked. I began walking up to Ordon and knelt right in front of him, so I did not have to yell when I spoke to him. "How much gold did this fox give you?" I asked.

Ordon paused and then dry coughed again before answering.

"Five King's gold now the other five when you are dead.."

Saber gasped.

"So, you only got five? I think my life would be worth more than ten pieces of metal!" A jolt of anger went through me. Before Heat Jr. and the others could act, I grabbed my sword. I pulled it so fiercely, it felt as if I pierced my palm with my nails. In one upward motion, I sliced Ordon in half. I figured he should be used to getting things in half by now.

"These things tend to be messy sometimes, but the desert is a dangerous place," Saber said.

Blaze and Saber dusted Heat Jr. and I off and hopped on their mounts. Before parting ways with us, Blaze said something that stuck with me.

"Whoever got that much coin on your head is dangerous. You two take care."

Heat Jr. sat his back to the well and watched them ride away.

"I'm glad you took care of him. I honestly don't have the strength to lift my sword." Heat Jr. had put on a show in front of his peers. Leadership was always questioned among those types.

"How much is 10 King's gold?" I asked.

Heat Jr. was silent; he seemed to be thinking in his head.

"One King's gold is valued at 100 gold coins. You could by a small town or part of a larger town with one King's gold. Someone doesn't just walk across that kind of coin; they already have it." Heat explained.

"You should rest up a bit more before we continue on."

Before I could even finish my sentence, Heat Jr. had already dozed off.

Heat Jr. slept for two more days before waking up. Whoever this person was must of known of a trance. I could not understand why a Foxfang would want me dead. My people did not value gold, so whoever he is must be an imposter. What little gold we did have we used for trading or traveling. Someone was pretending to be part of my tribe and aiming to break us apart for some reason. Or maybe it is someone hunting us down one by one…

Too many thoughts were running through my head. What I really needed to be doing was focusing on getting Heat Jr. and I to the Night Fox Tomb safely instead of a hundred other things. A smile found my face when I thought about how safely we had been getting to our destination. The Deathbringers and the Anger Asp: two things I had no control over, but somehow, I managed to get us to safety. The Anger Asp… If Ordon would have put it into the right bag, and it had bit me, things would have been a lot different. There were no mountains in the desert like at the Night Fox's tomb. Had I showed a display of my power like I did at the tomb in the desert, there would have been nothing left. The thought that someone knew that much about me and I knew nothing about them was haunting and had me on edge. Someone wanted me dead; I killed a not so innocent man for trying to follow an order. Now the order giver would be next.

When Heat Jr. woke up, my mind was clearer and more focused on things. I was focused on redeeming Heat Jr.'s father's name and taking back their castle. It seemed like a lot to take in, but it was what we needed to do, and we were right at their door. I looked in the well; the whole time, he was sleep. Every now and then, I thought I heard noises or saw a light, but it could have been my eyes playing tricks from looking in the dark. Whatever was on the other side of the well was not ready for a pair who had danced with DeathBringers or survived an Anger Asp bite.

"This well is probably bone dry. When I was younger, there was enough water in there to jump in and swim your way to the bottom," Heat added with a smile on his face.

I wanted to ask him what happens to his hair when it got wet… I'll save that question for another time.

"Then when I became older, I made this well a last resort escape route. I made it for my father…. Not me. When I first realized what it meant to be King, I always feared for my father's safety. If you look closely, you can see where I dug in my own steps to get up and down."

Heat Jr. pointed to the stone walls. I saw the steps now, but I did not see them the whole time I was looking while he was sleeping. A smile found my face.

"I've been thinking, what should we do with horses?" I asked.

Heat Jr. petted them both.

"Horses are smart. They will find their way."

Heat was right. These two horses were indeed very bright; they proved it by sticking by our sides. I did not doubt that our paths would cross again. I think I was starting to get attached to Etch. I hugged him tight then set him free.

"Are you ready for this?" Heat Jr. asked. I replied with a nod. Heat Jr. summoned a small fire ball in his hand. It burned bright for a moment, then turned to a cloud of smoke.

"I'm nowhere near full strength, but we are a bit behind schedule, wouldn't you say?"

We took the things we could not go without and then headed down. Heat Jr. went first and then I followed him. The walls of the well were dry. There had been some time since water been there. Heat Jr. stopped climbing.

"Be sure not to speak. We don't know who or what is down here."

As we continued our way, down I thought about Heat Jr.'s condition. He was not at full health, yet he wanted to press on. I tried to read him; I did not know what kept him going at this moment. I did not know if it was anger, duty, or purpose.

Heat Jr. kept a steady pace. Climbing had been one of the things I did best living in the forest, but we always climbed up. Never really climbed down. There was a first time for everything. I am not sure how much further, but Heat Jr. came to a stop. I did not want to ask if he was hurt because he said not to speak. Moments later, he looked up at me and smiled, then continued down.

I followed on after and paused where he did. When I put my hand in the step, the stone was very warm. It frightened me, and I almost lost my grip. This must be the entrance of his kingdom. There must be some type of enchantment in this area. Heat Jr. was saying a few words of prayer when he touched this stone. I had no words to say. I looked down at Heat Jr. and shook my head to let him know that I understood.

We were down in the well far enough that the light at the top was about the size of a dining plate. Heat Jr. stopped climbing again. We had climbed a great distance but nowhere compared to Tree Top Canopy. When I looked down at him, he motioned that he was letting go and was going to reach for his sword. Before he let go, he put his back to the well's wall.

He put on the Crown of Nightmares and covered up his flames. He let go and dropped, disappearing from my sight. I let go and followed behind Heat Jr.

I landed and knelt on the ground beside Heat Jr., and when I stood up, I grabbed my sword. This place was very dark, and for some reason made me feel uncomfortable. To the left of us was a room that was caved in by rocks, and in front of us was the path that would lead us to the castle. The path was poorly lit by what it seemed like three candles on the wall.

We started to tiptoe down the hall. As we made our way to the first candle, there was a doorway that went to our right. We both stopped in our tracks when we heard voices. It appeared to be two men on watch duty, making small talk and laughing. Heat Jr. slid alongside the wall until he was at the opening of the doorway. Heat Jr. poked his head around the corner to see what were up against. He motioned to me that there were two men sitting down, and to go for the throat. Heat Jr. counted on his fingers and mouthed the words, "One… two… Three!"

On the count of three, we both leaped out and took the two by surprise. Heat Jr. took the one on the left, and I took the one on the right. First thing I did was grab the unexpected man's mouth with my left hand and slid the blade of my sword to his throat. He put up a fight for a moment, but when his blood painted the walls, the fighting stopped. Heat Jr. and I both were breathing heavy. This was our first lives. There is no telling how many more we will have to take.

I started to make my way down the hallway the two men were guarding. Heat Jr. shook his head no and motioned me back down the hallway with the three candles. As we made our way down the hallway, we moved swiftly and quietly. When we made it to the second candle, we were in the middle of the hallway. The last candle was at the end of the hallway, and then it turned left.

When we got close to the end of the hallway, Heat Jr. slowed down his steps. There were more voices just around the corner. Heat

Jr. poked his head around swiftly, looked back at me, and signaled three fingers. He poked his head around again. This time he pointed to himself, telling me he was going to take out two of them, and I was to take the one on the left. I nodded my head in understanding. Before we went, Heat Jr. made his sword glowing red hot. On his three count, he jumped out. I was right behind him. We acted quickly and did not make a sound. Their bodies were lifeless before they even hit the ground.

Heat Jr. started to search the bodies of the men who lay before us. There was a cell around the corner full of prisoners. He was looking for the keys. I bent down to give him a hand. I spotted them in no time. I gave them a gentle jingle and nodded my head toward the cell. We darted for a cell. As we darted for the cell, sleepy-eyed prisoners' eyes opened wide open. I found humor in the fact that a Foxfang and man wearing a Crown of Nightmares was breaking prisoners out of the cell. Many of them maybe had never even heard of us Foxfang, and the others were just shocked in general, which made me smile.

When we got to the cage, voices began to whisper. The cell was full of about a dozen of Heat Jr.'s kinsmen who were starved and looked as if they have not seen sunlight in Maker knows how long. They were definitely in no shape to be fighting. I looked over at Heat Jr., and he gave me a nod.

When I put the keys to the cell's keyhole, everyone in the cell backed themselves to the wall in fear. The gate swung open, and Heat Jr. motioned to follow him.

He led us all back down the way we came. When we got to the fallen guards, the prisoners were quick to pick up their weapons. Heat Jr. led us all the way back to the doorway where the two guards were. Again, weapons were acquired by the prisoners. The doorway went downstairs. As soon as we turned the corner to go down the steps, there were two guards at the bottom of the stairs. We did not have the element of surprise this time. Heat Jr. and I led the assault. The two guards gave it their all, but it was not enough. As soon as we made our way passed the fallen, there was another set of steps followed by more guards at the bottom of them. In front of us stood six heavily armed knight. Equipped with spear in one hand shields in the other, guarding Heat Jr. family treasures.

Our two parties locked eyes. The tiny hallway where we stood was full of silence. Some of the prisoners' eyes were full of fear; the others' full of vengeance and rage. We did manage to put a surprised look on a few of the knights' faces. We had the knights outnumbered, but the prisoners were starved and in no shape to fight.

Before Heat Jr. and I could act, the prisoners rushed past us and started attacking the knights wildly. The knights' moves were swift and well-practiced, but it was still no match for the prisoners. The once silent hallway was now full of shouting and the clanking of metal.

Although the knights were well-trained, they were still no match for the prisoners who seemed to be somewhat trained. What they lacked in training, they made up for it with their numbers and their rage. The prisoners ended the guards quickly and then picked up their weapons. When they picked up the weapons, they pointed them at us and quickly circled around Heat Jr. and I.

"What is the meaning of this? Why have you freed us? Are you here to help yourself to family treasure? one of the prisoners asked.

Heat Jr. slowly put his hands up to take off the Crown of Nightmares. The prisoners dropped their weapons and down to a knee, quicker than they picked up the weapons.

"The King..." they all whispered with their heads bowed.

The eldest man of the bunch reached up and touched Heat Jr.'s face.

"I do not believe my eyes," he said to Heat Jr.

"Bavris, believe your eyes. It is me," Heat Jr. spoke with joy.

"So, you're not here for gold. Your here for..."

The room went silent. Many heads nodded, for they all knew he spoke of Heat Jr.'s father.

"I intend on ending this once and for all. Take what you need now. When this over, all the riches down here will be yours," Heat Jr. pointed at the collection of treasure.

Those words were music to the prisoners' ears. Their faces glowed like the first day of harvest. They did not look like they had much in them, but the will of their king is what gave them the strength to keep going.

As I looked around, I saw we were surrounded by hundreds of years of family history. Helmets, swords, spears, axes, shields. If you could think of it, it was in here. Bags of gold with coins stuffed to the top sat in one corner of the room, stacked taller than I stood. There was a wall full of family portraits. The one that stood out the most was the largest. It touched the ceiling and almost touched the floor. I thought to myself that this must have been the first King of the Flames. All the faces had family resemblance, except for his. He was also the only face who did not wear a head of flames. I walked over to the wall of portraits and stood under the large painting. As I got closer, I realized there was no frame. The picture was actually painted on the wall. I looked over at Heat Jr.; he was helping a young man fasten his armor tight. I wanted to ask him about the portrait, but now did not seem like the time to talk about such things.

Sniff… sniff… I smelled around the portrait. There was magic in the paint! I took a few more sniffs. The smell was unfamiliar. I could not tell what kind of magic it was, but it was there.

As everyone went around arming themselves, I sought for something that would possibly give me the edge in the battle yet to come. After all, Heat Jr. did say to take what we needed. I needed something I could hide and use without the enemy seeing it coming. There had to be some type of throwing weapon amongst these treasures. Tucked away in the corner, there was a target. This target was full of arrows, knives, and axes. Whoever threw them was truly a good marksman. Heat Jr. walked over to me with a smile on his face.

"I see you stumbled upon ranged weapons. We Scorchis don't breed to many marksmen, but the few we have had are always dead on," Heat Jr. said.

Getting a better look at the target, I noticed all the objects in the target made an "X."

"Indeed, whoever placed those was a true marksman."

"A markswoman did these," Heat Jr. said as he pulled out a knife. "These belonged to Gillian. She was said to have the steadiest hand on the mountain."

Heat Jr. handed me two of Gillian's throwing knives. They were what I needed. Light weight, small, barely noticed, and sharp. I threw one of the knives, and I landed just under the target.

"Not bad," Heat Jr. said while shaking his head in approval. "Then we are ready?" Heat Jr. held his hand up and the small room grew quiet. "Thank you," was all he could say.

Heat Jr. rushed us back to the cells. When we got there, the once prisoners spat at its gates. There was a heavy metal door next to the cells. Heat Jr. put his back to it and looked at all of us. He nodded his head then he turned his head to listen for noises. My heart was beating out of my chest. I could feel my body start to sweat, and my grip get tighter on my sword. We came this far; there was no going back. Heat Jr. closed his eyes and took a few deep breaths.

The metal door creaked open slowly. Heat Jr. walked out first, then me, and after that, everyone followed. We were now in Heat Jr.'s throne room. The throne looked as if it was boulder with a sitting place carved into it. In front of the throne, one on each side, were what looked like fireplaces made of stone. The lower part of the fireplace came about up to the waist. Then there was a nice sized space where the flame went, and it was open on all sides. On top of that was a higher part of the stone fireplaces that connected to the top of the room.

A set of stairs was to our right. It went from one side of the room to the other, so that the two sets of steps met in the middle. The upstairs had a door on each of the four walls. This place was marvelous. The walls were made of red mountain rocks that I had never seen before. The pillars were made of the same rocks, but they had been polished so much that you could see white veins throughout them. The floors were polished the same, it looked like a glossy sea of fire. There was a large red carpet with white trim that went from the front door all the way to the throne. On the wall behind the throne was a large banner red with white trim that had an open flame in a darker shade of red on it.

"Come out, you coward!" Heat Jr. shouted. Heat Jr.'s words bounced off the walls of the silent room. Every member of the party tried to hold Heat Jr. back, but we could not. He darted to the middle of the room. We all followed behind him. We made haste and wasted no time huddling into a circle with our backs touching one another. As we surrounded by so much silence, you could hear nothing but deep breaths and the heart beating inside your chest. We waited and still no one came.

"Do you think they left the castle?" one of the men said.

"Quiet!" Heat Jr. said. You could hear that his jaw was clenched, and there was anger in his voice. "They are here. He is here. He would not leave with unfinished business to attend."

We waited some more… Still nothing.

One of the men fixed his mouth as if he were going to speak, but before the words came out, Heat. Jr shook his head no.

I too, started to think that the men left but kept quiet. I did not want to upset Heat Jr. more than he already was. I could not tell if he was angry or scared.

A noise came from a distance. We all looked around to see if we could tell which direction it came from. The noise came again, and I still could not tell which direction it came from. A smile came to Heat Jr.'s face.

"They come now."

As I listened closer, I could hear that sound we were hearing was marching. The marching started slow. Then began to get faster. Everyone was looking at the doors to see which direction they were coming from. It took me a moment to notice that they were not coming from one side. They were coming at us from all sides.

The door over the entrance opened first. Five men rushed out with swords that looked as if they were twice the size of the man holding it in one hand and a very large armored glove made from metal that went all the way up to their shoulder in the other. Where the elbow was there was a large cluster of spikes. Both side doors opened next. Men with swords and shields piled out the door and looked down on us. Finally, the door over the throne opened. Six men with spears ran down the stairs, three of them on each side. The first in line stopped at the bottom of the steps and pointed their spears at us. I was close enough that I could see into one of the men's eyes. The next in line stood a few steps up behind the other men. Just far enough that their spears were not touching the man in front of him. The last in line stood at the top of the stairs.

We were outnumbered and surrounded. There was a handful of us and about three hands full of them. They stood motionless, watching us. Off in the distance, you could hear metal boots walking on the stone floor. Someone was coming out of the hallway of the middle door. Out came a large bald man with a beard full of flames. He wore the same style of armor as Heat Jr. did, but his armor looked as if it was made of stone. He had two of the armored gloves, and no sword. The armor gloves looked like gauntlets with shields on them at the wrist area. He stood taller than anyone, and his chest was rounder than anyone else's in the room. This must be the man that killed Heat Jr.'s father.

"Quite the welcoming for me."

When Heat Jr. spoke those words, the silence felt as if it got quieter. One of the men of the steps kneeled where he was when he saw Heat Jr. face. The bald man smiled and walked over to the kneeled man.

"I thought the next time I'd see your face in here it would surely be on a spike," he laughed while kicking the kneeled man down the stairs. The man landed at our feet and made a loud crash when he hit the floor.

"I know some of you have misplaced loyalty, but if you put your weapons down now, I will not bring you any harm."

The throne room began to fill with laughter.

We were outnumbered, and yet Heat Jr. still thought we had a fighting chance. Heat Jr. was surely bluffing. The men who were with us were starved and could barely stand on their own. Heat Jr. was mad if he thought one of ours could take out at least three of theirs.

"You truly wish to follow a man who did not have to fight to get to where he is?"

The room went silent, and a few weapons dropped to the ground. Heat Jr.'s bluff was truly working.

"Jasper the Red, I'm awake! Not even the lowest of guttersnipes would butcher a man in his sleep."

A few more weapons dropped to the ground, but there were still more weapons in hands than there were on the ground.

Jasper the Red started walking down the stairs.

"Your father would always use his words and not his actions, that is why he is dead. Enough with the words. Show me some actions," Jasper said.

Heat Jr. stood in the middle of the room waiting for Jasper to make his way down the steps. The rest of us backed ourselves to the entrance of the throne room door. The men above us gripped the rails with anticipation. When Jasper was on the ground level, Heat Jr. pulled his sword. Heat followed him with the sword until he stopped walking. Heat Jr. put both of his hands on his sword. Jasper put both of his hands up and took his fighting stance.

Jasper charged at Heat Jr., swinging his fists wildly. Heat Jr. showed off by not swinging or blocking; just moved out of the way. Jasper went in for another charge. This time, Heat Jr. met fist to sword every time Jasper swung. When Jasper swung a mighty blow towards Heat Jr.'s head, there was no blocking it with the sword. Heat Jr. jumped backwards. Before he could get good footing, Jasper swung the same fist that nearly took Heat Jr.'s head off so hard to the ground at Heat Jr.'s feet. The blow was so mighty, it broke the mountain rock on the floor and sent chunks flying. It was impressive to see how quickly Jasper moved the large gloves.

As Heat Jr. jumped back to dodge this attack, he extended his body as much as he could to try and kick Jasper in the face, but he could not land the kick. A smile found its way to Jasper's face.

Heat Jr. ran in for an assault. He leaped in the air to try and kick Jasper in the face again. Jasper crossed his metal gloves to block his face. As soon as Heat Jr.'s feet hit the ground, he started swing like he did not have a purpose. Jasper was able to block every time Heat Jr. swung. By pushing Heat Jr.'s sword back when he swung, Jasper broke Heat Jr.'s rhythm. This caused one of Heat Jr.'s hands to come off his sword.

Before Heat Jr. could realize his mistake, Jasper delivered a nasty blow to Heat Jr.'s midsection that dropped him to the ground instantly.

Heat Jr. was quick to hop to his feet. Heat Jr. realized his mistake. Heat Jr. had also realized Jasper was not going to hold nothing back. Heat Jr. was indeed holding back. The display of power Heat Jr. showed in the desert was a path of death and destruction in the blink of an eye. What I saw before me now was a piss-poor effort of combat, if I had ever seen one compared to what Heat Jr. did in the desert.

Heat Jr. swung quickly at Jasper. The swings he had just performed did no damage to Jasper. Heat Jr. was making sparks come off Jasper's armor. He made the sparks go into Jasper's face, and for a moment Jasper could not see. A moment was all Heat Jr. needed to thrust his shoulder into Jasper's chest and knock him off his feet. Before Jasper could even hit the ground, Heat Jr. was in the air. Ready to plunge his sword through Jasper's chest. Somehow Jasper grabbed the sword and Heat Jr. missed. This put Jasper on the ground with Heat Jr.'s sword closer to his face than to his chest. Jasper struggled to get Heat Jr. off him. Heat Jr. was hammering the hilt of his sword with his fist. Each time Heat Jr. hit his sword, he brought it closer to Jasper's face. Jasper kicked one of Heat Jr.'s legs away. This drove Heat Jr.'s sword straight down. Jasper was able to make it out of the way: for a man his size he moved like a hooftin.

Jasper stood up and grabbed his face. Heat Jr.'s sword made contact with Jasper's face, and a narrow stream of blood flowed from his cheek. Jasper jumped in the air with his hands together to come down with hammering fists. Heat Jr. did not move out of the way like he should of. He put his sword up to block the fist, but as soon as they made contact Jasper put his boot to Heat Jr.'s chest. This sent Heat Jr. back flying. Jasper flung one of his gloves at Heat Jr.. He was not able to move out of the way, so he caught it the best he could before it crushed his face. The glove set on top of Heat Jr. with his hands under it and elbows pinned to the ground. It was so heavy Heat Jr. could not move it. Jasper wasted no time charging at Heat Jr. while he could not move. Jasper jumped in the air for another hammer fist, but this time with one glove. Before Jasper reached his target, the flames stood up on Heat Jr.'s head like I'd never seen before. That was followed by a larger burst of flames. Jasper went one way; his glove went the other.

Heat Jr. was on his feet and headed for Jasper. Jasper looked over at his glove and darted for it. Before he could get to it, Heat Jr. brought the flames to his sword like he did in the desert. I snorted under my breath and shook my head. Heat Jr. was testing Jasper like he did me at Dagger Tip, but this time putting someone to the test nearly killed him. And yet he was still holding back. While we were in the desert Heat Jr.'s moves could not be matched, and his power could not be bested. Now that I think of it, Heat Jr. was under the effects of an Anger Asp. Heat Jr. was not in total control of his actions. If standing in front of the man who killed your father did not make Heat Jr. angry, I did not know what would.

Heat Jr. let Jasper grab his other glove. When the glove was on Jasper made the flames in his bread light up and that was followed by his gloves flaming like Heat Jr.'s sword. A smile came to my face as I thought if Shadow were here, he would say, "The both of them were having a cock measuring contest," cause that's what the two were doing. This was a fight to the death, but they were acting as if it was just a test of power. Someone had to win. They both would not leave this room alive. As they exchanged blows, it would seem like Jasper would be the victor. They way Jasper pounded Heat Jr.'s face repeatedly led my mind to think what would happen if Heat Jr. fell in battle. I know for a fact that I would be the first to step in and cross blades with Jasper. Would the prisoners jump to my side and act, or would they cower back under Jasper's boot? Would the men upstairs rain down fury on the king's men or the one who would cause harm to the king's men. The uncertainty of those unanswered questions caused my grip to become tighter on my sword.

Heat Jr. stood in front of Jasper beaten and looked like he could barely stand on his own two feet. As long if Heat Jr. could breathe, this fight was not over. The two ran at each other; Heat Jr. planted his feet and swung for Jasper's head. Jasper spun out of the way while standing on one foot. When he planted his other foot, he landed another blow to Heat Jr. midsection. Heat Jr. was in a daze, he took a few stutter steps back and then Jasper charged again. Jasper pushed Heat Jr. to the wall by his neck; Heat Jr.'s feet dangled in the air as Jasper tried to punch his face. Heat Jr. twisted and turned his neck to avoid the punches while being choked. The first few, he was able to miss. When Jasper landed one, it was because Heat Jr. lowered his head and Jasper punched his forehead. It definitely hurt Heat Jr. more than Jasper, but it gave Heat

Jr. a little time to think. Heat Jr. put his feet on the wall and then kicked off. A blast of flames from his feet sent the two flying across the throne room. Heat Jr. got up slowly, sword in one hand, ball of flames in the other. Before Heat Jr. had his feet firmly planted, Jasper was on his way. Jasper sent his fist sailing towards Heat Jr.; Heat Jr. did not budge, just lifted the fist with the fire ball. Heat Jr. blocked the punch with the ball of fire that he turned into a flaming shield. Jasper struck the shield, again. Again. Again. Nothing happened. It was at that moment, I realized Jasper was a brute. Magic was not his strongest leg to stand on. Hand to hand close range was where he was keeping the fight this whole time. Heat Jr. had the upper hand this whole time and did not know it. How long would it take Heat Jr. to notice?

The two circled around the room. Heat Jr.'s movements were sluggish, but he still somehow had some fight in him. Jasper wasted no time and shortened the distance between them. When the fists started raining down on Heat Jr., his shield was there to withstand the fury. How much longer would the shield hold up against the earth trembling blows delivered by Jasper? The door to victory seemed to be shutting on Heat Jr.. Each blow brought him closer to his knees.

"Arrgggghhh!" Jasper let out an ear pounding roar. Heat Jr. stabbed his sword through Jasper's arm where he had the most muscle. As the two stood there frozen for what seemed like forever, I realized that this fight was near over. Heat Jr. was not moving because he was saving what little energy he had left. Jasper was not moving because I am sure he was in a world of hurt. Their next moves were crucial, or their last move.

Heat Jr. flicked his wrist and turned his blade. Jasper let out another shout and kicked Heat Jr. away from him. Heat Jr. was able to recover from it quickly, but Jasper was left where he stood. Holding his arm as the blood gushed from the womb, Jasper acted fast, throwing both of his gloves at Heat Jr. He threw one high, and he threw one low. Heat Jr. either had to block the high one and take the lower one or, block the lower one and take the high one. When the time came to act, Heat Jr. was too tired and slow to move. Heat Jr. could not move out the way fast enough, so he was pummeled by both of the gloves. Heat Jr. was out cold. Jasper staggered his way over to his one of his gloves and picked it up.

My already clenched sword slowly wormed its way out my sheath. Few of the men around me heard my movements and slowly did the same thing. I was trying not to be heard because I wanted the upper hand on Jasper; he would not suspect me coming if he could not hear me. The fact that a few of the other men did the same let me know we were running at the same pace.

Jasper brought his glove above his head to drop it down on Heat Jr. One of the prisoners started running at Jasper before I could. Before we could get to Jasper, he had already dropped it towards Heat Jr.'s motionless body. Before Jasper's glove hit Heat Jr., there was a flash of flames that covered Heat Jr.'s body. Moments later, a bigger flash of flames came from Heat Jr. and pushed Jasper back. Heat Jr.'s body was floating in front of us. The flashes of flames we were seeing were wings.

The Phoenix had possessed Heat Jr.'s body and the wings were sticking out his back. Floating in front of Jasper was Heat Jr.'s sleeping body and a set of massive flaming wings. In one flap of the wings, Jasper was turned into a pile of ash. The wings spread wide open, and in one spin, everyone who stood on the steps and the floor above us was turned into a pile of ash. The Phoenix sprung itself from Heat Jr.'s body, and he fell to the ground. The Phoenix let out a loud squawk and then exploded straight up and through the roof of the building and flew away. When the Phoenix busted through the roof, the castle began to slowly melt, almost like the wax of a candle. My mouth was left wide open, and I was speechless from what I had just saw.

One of the prisoners ran and grabbed Heat Jr. and brought him outside. I was still in shock from the display of power I had just laid my eyes on and was still standing inside watching the castle slowly burn. I knew Heat Jr. was the Prince of Flames, but I could not understand how he did these things while being unconscious; violently killing people and then peacefully burning the castle to the ground. The stones smolder like paper to the ground, nothing fell or tumbled. It would seem this place had been cleansed. I finally walked outside. We all gathered around Heat Jr., sat, and watched the castle burn. The sun was up, but it was on its way down. The way the two semi-lit the sky was very peaceful to me made me feel like nothing could go wrong. I was naive to have any thoughts of there not being more people like Jasper walking these lands. Just looking at this sunset gave me hope that things could be good.

"Zek!" I heard in a familiar voice. It was Heat Jr., and he was alive and well. The sun had gone down and the castle had burned down to the steps. I must have dozed off watching the flames.

"Look down there." He pointed down the mountain. There was a fire being started, and a tiny smoke cloud above it. "Your bandits are starting up their forge," Heat Jr. said. He was pointing at the Night Fox's tomb.

"I know it doesn't look far away, but it's only about a half day's run. It would be a lot quicker if we did not have to worry about rocky and always changing edges. These mountain paths aren't what they use to be. We need to travel light. Leave behind anything that will slow us down."

The men began to tear off the armor that they did not get a chance to use. They were damn near wearing just boots, pants and a sword. He really meant for us all to run there.

"Are you sure you're able to make it there?" I asked.

Heat Jr. laughed ever so slightly.

"Are you sure you can keep up?"

I thought to myself, *Another race?* Then I saw Krinkel's smile.

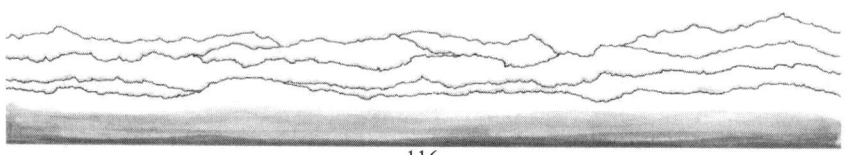

I could see the Night Fox's tomb; we were coming upon it quickly. The tomb was a large fox skull. I remember the place being different in my vision. The entrance to the tomb was at the fox's mouth, which was open midway. The two eyes were windows; where the snout was, there was a large balcony carved. It was all carved from white stone. Or could this really have been the skull of a fox? The bandits still had their fires burning. I did not know what I was dragging Heat Jr. and his men into. So many things were running through my mind, but these men were my Brothers of the Flame. That meant we would protect one another, no matter what we faced inside the tomb.

Before we even entered, I smelled a familiar smell. There was another Foxfang near. Could it be the rogue Fox Fang Aggrippa spoke of was here now? I would meet him face-to-face and put an end to his madness. When we first ran in, I realized we were outnumbered. They had a trip wire set up at the entrance. I stepped on it. The mouth of the fox shut, killing the last two men who entered instantly.

When the bandits laid their eyes on us, they began to scatter. Some fought and stood their ground. Others grabbed whatever they could get their greasy hands and tried to make it to the entrance. The first bandit that ran up to me and tried to take my head off with an axe. His movements were sloppy. I did not even waste time drawing my sword, I just cast *Fox Fire* in his face. Four men fell in line where that one had stood. Before I could even think about what to do next, Heat Jr. threw his flaming sword, dropping them instantly. Behind him, two more of ours picked up the fallen men's spears and backed their backs to the entrance. They were making sure none of these bastards made it out.

Every step you took, there was either bone or some type of weapon on the ground. The bandits really worked this place over, leaving no tomb unturned. The chair where the Night Fox sat in my vision lied on the ground in many pieces. Many years of Foxfang art and even more generations of my people's history laid on the ground. The fact that someone would dishonor the dead in this type of manner angered me greatly. The bandits would be lucky to make it out of here without me laying my hands on them.

"Zek!" Heat Jr. shouted and pointed at a person hooded in black robs. It was the rogue Foxfang! And he had just picked up a bag of weapons from the forge.

"That bag does not leave this tomb!" I shouted loud enough everyone heard me. The whole room's attention shifted to the bag and its handler. I picked up the closest thing to me that I could throw at him. It was a round metal shield. I threw it, aiming right for his legs. The agile bastard was fast enough to hop on it and off, then off the wall to get out of the way. Two of ours jumped at him to tackle him, he dropped them both; one did not get back up. Heat Jr. was able to grab him briefly, but he was able to shake himself free. When the hooded man shook himself free, he dropped one of the weapons out of the bag. He did not stop to pick it up. His load was lighter, and able to move about much faster.

He was heading up stairs. Before he could get up there two of ours were waiting for him. I was not too far from behind him. The men had their weapons drawn, but when they went in to attack the hooded man pulled a sword from the bag. They both swung at the same time. It was like he knew what they were going to do before they even made their moves. The first blade that came his way he dipped down lower and stabbed clean through the man's lungs. The second sword that came his way he deflected back by spinning the sword away from him. When he came back around, that is when he plunged his sword into the chest of his enemy. The hooded man looked at me, put the sword away, and kept running. I threw my sword at the wall right in front of his face. Forcing him to turn around and fight, but I did not have a weapon now. I tried to kick his head off, but he was able to lean his body back and out of the way. Using my fist, I swung, not as hard as I could. Just to see if I could land a punch.

I threw three punches, and none of them landed. My first punch was dodged just by him stepping out of the way. The second one went right past his face. Just when I thought I was going to send him into the Lillies, I drew back for a punch, too far back. In the time it took me to bring my fist back, he had enough time to kick my arm to the wall and stopping my punch. In the same motion a back spin, kicking me in the chest. Damn near knocking the wind out of me. He was indeed faster than me, but what really impressed me was the way he launched himself off my chest and back down the stairs. My animal instincts kicked in, and I was on all fours chasing after him.

Before I could get downstairs, he had passed the bag off to one of his men and was headed towards the entrance.

"Heat!" I shouted and pointed at the bag.

By the time Heat Jr. had a chance to see what I was pointing at the bag had changed hands once again. I looked around for the hooded man, he was trying to open the mouth on the tomb. He was not going to get it open if I had anything to do with it. Out in the distance, there was a familiar screeching sound. It was the Phoenix! He came flying in the tomb through the eye-shaped window and circled above us. Everyone stopped and looked at this magnificent creature move a about the tomb like a feather. I had many questions, but no time to ask. The time I spent looking at the Phoenix should have been spent ending this madness.

The hooded man looked at the Phoenix, but it did not take long for him to focus his mind back on escaping. His back was to the wall. When I ran up to him, I tried to kick his head through the wall. He moved out the way. In fact, he was so fast, I lost count of the numbers of kicks. He managed to dodge them all and move past me. He was trying to make his way back to the bag. Heat Jr. had his hands full; there was still more of them than us, it was easier for them to move the bag about. The bandits dropped the bag back into the hooded man hands, and that left him and I standing face-to-face. I could not see his eyes because he was wearing the hood so low. I reached for the bag. He finally drew his sword on me. Before I could act, he had lunged forward and stabbed right beside me. At first, I smiled because his aim was off, then I noticed he was not aiming for me. He was aiming for a bandit who tried to stab me in the back. He wanted me alive? The hooded man put the sword back into the bag. I swung at the hooded man like my life depended on it. Each time I tried to punch or grab the agile bastard; he was able to parry all attacks. We stood face-to-face again. This time, I was out of breath. He made things seem as if he was not even trying. I went in one more time. Before I could get in striking distance, he crouched down, and I was met by his leather foot to my stomach. I took a few steps back, and he tried to knock me down with a leg sweep. I was able to avoid that, but the bag came around right after his leg. I did not expect him to use the bag as a weapon. Thus the bag hit me behind the knees and sent my body to the ground violently.

I laid on my back with the wind knocked out of me, looking up at the Phoenix. The Phoenix stopped circling. He flapped his wings once, and bodies began to burn like they did at the castle. I sat myself up and saw that the hooded man was walking slowly away as if he was taunting me. There was a bow and arrow at my feet. I was not the best archer, but I gave it a shot. The hooded man did not even look back or budge. I shot the arrow. He put his back towards the entrance wall and watched the arrow fly by him. I was out of arrows, so I picked up one of the bones on the ground and shot it at him. When I released the bone from the bow, it was like I casted *Fox Fire*. A large flaming fox was chasing after the hooded man. The hooded man slid on his knees, and the fox went right over his head. I missed my target again and blasted away the teeth that stopped him from leaving the tomb. The hooded man waited for the smoke to clear. When it did, he stepped out the tomb looked back and waved with his middle finger.

The hooded man whistled, and a horse came running. He threw the bag on first, then hopped on and began to ride off. I picked up another bone about the size of a spear and ran to the balcony. The hooded man was already a great distance away, but I threw it anyways. When I let the bone go this time, it was as if I cast *Fox Fire*. Only this time the fox was much larger and traveled much faster. To my surprise, the fox actually traveled out to the hooded man. What surprised me even more is when the fox reached the hooded man. The agile bastard—in the blink of an eye—jump and did a spinning kick, kicking the fox away from him and landed back on his horse. When he landed, the hood came off. The rogue Foxfang was a woman. She rode off with a bag of weapons made of our ancestors' bones.